The Bookbinder's Brother

ROSANNE DINGLI

A collection with this title was first published by Jacobyte Books, Australia 2003
The stories in this book appeared in A Great Intimacy (2011) and Encore (2011), two collections of stories by this author, both now out of print.

Yellow Teapot Books
ISBN-13: 978-1479254996
ISBN-10: 1479254991

Cover image
John the Bookbinder – a picture painted with coffee – courtesy Angel and Andy of justcoffeeart.com

This edition designed and set in Palatino Linotype

Also by Rosanne Dingli

Death in Malta
According to Luke
Camera Obscura
The Day of the Bird
Counting Churches – The Malta Stories

Rosanne Dingli is an award-winning Western
Australian author. Her work has appeared in
print and on the Internet since 1985. She has
worked in various publishing roles, and has
lectured in writing. For more information, visit
rosannedingli.com

For Ramon and Ravenna

The stories in this book appeared, in slightly different forms, in *The Bookbinder's Brother*, published by Jacobyte Books in 2003.

Walking into the Sea won first prize at the Fellowship of Australian Writers Lyndal Hadow Awards, Western Australia, 1998.

The House with its feet in the Sea first appeared in Reader's World, Western Australia, 1995

Cacti was commended at the Tasmanian Fellowship of Australian Writers Awards, 1987

Dancing Words was highly commended at the Let's Write Competition, Victoria 1993

Playing from Memory appeared in Sibling Stories 2, (edited by Barbara Holland) published by Fremantle Arts Centre Press in 1997.

A Great Intimacy won the 1994 Springvale Award.

Il Funerale di Un Vescovo was very highly commended at the 1998 Lyndal Hadow Awards.

The Bookbinder's Brother appeared in Voices, Canberra 1993.

Twenty Minutes, Two Years appeared in Voices, Canberra, in 1992.

Contents

What critics say about Rosanne Dingli's fiction:

The Bookbinder's Brother
'Plain titles belie the intricacy of these carefully crafted tales, as they explore the relationship between past and present selves and belonging – to a person, to a job, a landscape, or a set of values.'
Dennis Haskell
Editor of *Westerly*,
Professor of English
University of Western Australia

Death in Malta
'… you gave the island and its people real substance, the exuberant sounds of the fireworks, the smells of the tenements, the steep narrow alleys and the clip-clop of the pony's feet on the roadway.   All give intense flavour.'
Ian Mathie
Author of *Bride Price, Man in a Mud Hut* and *Man of Passage and other stories out of Africa*

According to Luke
'A remarkable combination of star-crossed romance and international thriller. Absorbing.'
Janet Woods
Author of *Salting the Wound* and *Paper Doll*

Counting Churches

'I really loved reading this book - I saw my birth place thorough the eye of a Maltese person who has lived here a while ago. The stories are all superb, the descriptions exceptional, and you can almost see and hear the characters come alive before your very eyes. I will certainly be reading more of this author. '
Whiskey
Amazon.com

Making a Name
'Dingli has the ability of a masterful storyteller to maintain a flow and pace that keep the reader enchanted and calmly waiting for the next devastation. 'Making a Name' was definitely my favorite story and deserves the title of the book. It is beautifully rendered and eerily mysterious. … 'Making a Name' ranks with the best stories I have ever read. Dingli is able to achieve something many writers (and fisherman) can't, she snags gently, she maintains tension, and she gives just enough line to keep you hooked.'
Dan Mader
Author of *The Biker* and *Joe Café*

Camera Obscura

'Dingli proves once again that she is capable of producing well researched and detailed storylines, which hook you from the off and pull you along at a fast pace until a conclusion is reached in epic proportions. Her style of prose, layers of interesting characters and plot complexity sit comfortably within the vibrantly colourful depictions of her chosen European destinations, making this psychological thriller an action packed read …'
Andria Saxelby
The Kindle Book Review

The Bookbinder's Brother

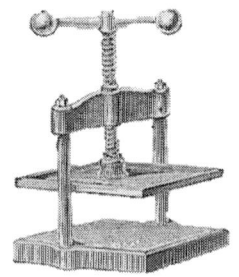

The Bookbinder's Brother

We could hear Serge's chainsaw going in the cleft of the valley. Eric stood as close to me as our axes allowed.

'I keep waiting for him to stop,' he said, and shook his head. 'To pause, even – but he goes on and on.'

The sound of the saw continued un-interrupted and we craned our necks towards its buzzing in the forest, like horses. We had become like horses, hauling logs and obeying Serge with hardly a whinny.

'He can work,' I said.

Eric nodded and wiped off more sweat. 'He likes that new machine.'

The break we cut was wide enough for a tractor now. The timber would serve for the barn. 'When do we start on the barn?' I was very impatient. I wanted to know how long it would be before I did anything else but fell trees and shave bark off prostrate cylinders of new wood.

'Soon as those fellows arrive from Belfort.' He was breathless with exertion. 'They should have been here days ago.' He sat on a log. Its skin lay around him like huge pencil sharpenings. 'Look at my hands.' He sounded like a woman ruing dishpan skin. Eric was too urban for this. He should have been sitting at some desk, writing. He knew what I was thinking.

'I should be writing, you're thinking, eh?' He looked at me and wiped sweat off his chin. 'My brother's hands: now those are hands doing things that will last forever.'

I wondered what he meant. He listened for a pause in Serge's sawing. It never came.

'He never stops.'

I nodded.

'My brother is a bit like that, but he does stop, if you watch closely. His intervals are part of the work ... you know? He's thinking about the next step even when he pauses.'

'What does he do?' I was intrigued. But we heard crashing from the undergrowth. Two bays in a double rig dragged a chained triangle of logs whose ends were stained green from grass near the river. The horses' breathing filled the air. Then we heard the woman panting.

'Bonjour.' For a while, the noise of her team masked Serge's saw. When she passed we listened for him together. It was the sound of a dying fly at a kitchen window. Without enthusiasm, I reached for my axe. Eric's hand shot out and touched my wrist lightly.

'Listen!' A finger flew to his lips. The buzzing had stopped. Before he said anything else we heard it again, insistent as before.

'He jumped the stream,' Eric said.

I reached inside my breast pocket for the squashed packet of Gauloises. He took one and spent some time tapping it extremely lightly on the knee of his trousers, whose kneecaps were stiff and greenish, the seat threadbare. He had worked in them for six weeks. He said the war had made him used to things like that. Mine were no different. Serge said if we wanted to do washing we had to carry water up to the camp. It was hard enough lugging drinking water for us and the horses. We went for days without a wash or shave, save for a quick splash on our faces in the cold morning. Some Saturdays, when Serge disappeared, the rest of us got in the truck and went to the village where we had a shower and a decent shave. The skinflint who ran the baths made sure the water ran cold just as our joints were starting to feel elastic again. After a pastis at the café where the redhead worked, we all piled into the truck again.

'We should get her to wash our shirts,' someone once said, gesturing towards the girl, lifting his arm and wrinkling his nose as he tucked it into his armpit.

I thought she would wrinkle her own nose at that, but kept the sentiment to myself. None of us dared approach her except to order pastis. The redhead at the cafe: we all dreamed about her.

'What does your brother do?' I asked Eric again.

He looked at his broken shoes. 'What my father did. And my grandfather, and his father before him.' He opened his hands, palms upward, and peered at peeling callused skin on his hands. 'See, Walter?'

I was surprised to hear my name. No one had said it for months. My mother used to use it frequently, but the war took her.

He turned his hands over and stretched them, thumbs touching. One thumbnail was blackened and twisted. 'Hah!'

'And what is it they all did?'

'Hah!' He grimaced and exclaimed again.

'And where?' I asked.

'Colmar, of course.'

'Up here?' I flicked a thumb over my shoulder in disbelief.

I le nodded. There was something strange in his eyes, like regret, or animosity.

If my family were in Colmar I would not have spent my nights in a freezing shed with a stamped earth floor, pissing in the bush and having a shower every ten days in a tiny village with a short supply of hot water. Eric was crazy.

'I must be crazy, is what you're thinking.' He winked wryly.

I shoved another cigarette at him. He spent more time straightening the thing out, picking a loose thread of tobacco from one end with exaggerated patience, then lifted his head and listened for Serge's buzz. 'Near the railway.' His eyes were like slits, as he listened hard. 'And three or four stations away, Colmar, and my brother's shop.'

'What does he sell?' My curiosity was roused in a slow but certain way. I was now more intent on finding out why Eric spent his days in Spartan servility to a man like Serge, in clothes that could have walked away on their own, instead of being with his family. 'Why did you leave?' I wished I had a family in Colmar.

'There is a woman.' He spread his hands as if to say, naturally, there is a woman. The cigarette was stuck between his first two fingers as he turned his palms upward. A small thread of smoke curled round the blackened thumb. His eyes narrowed again. 'And she is nothing like the redhead you others think about, as you lie under Serge's old blankets and grunt and heave.' He mumbled something I did not catch. 'She has short hair like a boy, and a waist...' He held his hands to form a circle. Thumbs and forefingers almost touched. 'And strength in her arms to strangle a bull. She twists that screw like a man.'

'Screw?'

'The press screw.' He cocked his head to listen.

I noticed Serge's noise getting closer. 'He's crossed the road.'

5

It was hardly a road, but we called it that because the truck went on it as far as the village round the mountain. It was hardly a mountain, but we called it that because it hid the woman's farm and her goats. Soon we had to pretend to be hacking at bark again. Eric squinted at the sky. 'Nearly time, anyway.'

We were allowed to stop when the sun went down.

He went on softly, as if answering another of my questions. 'The books are put in large presses.'

I did not ask what books or he might stop talking. 'They're tied together with twine by Grammère. She has a thumb as wide and flat as a wooden spoon.'

I gave up trying to impose the concept of a narrative on what he was saying and just listened to the words.

'The pages are untrimmed and uncut. My brother brings them from the printer in a barrow. You should feel the weight of that paper! Sometimes it feels wet. You know? Laden with knowledge like water.'

I nodded.

'My brother makes the pages into books. Somehow, he makes sense of the writing and the page numbers and folds them together. He sews. He sews bundles of pages. He twists and folds, and hangs the pages on a frame, by their binding threads. Grammère – our mother's mother, she must be eighty – brings the twine. He has an awl as long as my middle finger.' He held it up. He held two fingers pinced together to suggest the sharpness of its

6

point. 'He sews,' he continued. 'Then he boils glue in the big pot ... no one remembers that pot not being there, you know? It's been hanging over that stove for centuries, its rim is caked with old glue. Dribbles from the bones of old horses. He dips brushes into the pot and tests the glue. I tell you, it smells like hell, binds like eternity. Then the press – they turn the screw together. Shoulders like a boy, she has. If I could touch them, those shoulders, they would be like a boy's.'

I asked more questions but he did not hear me. He forgot I was there. He created a picture for me of books being bound, and I wondered what a woman with the haircut and shoulders of a boy was doing there. I was shaken out of my wonder. Serge burst through the undergrowth with a startling crash. 'Hey! You two finished for the day?'

We had not noticed the buzzing had stopped. 'There is stew at the cabin,' our boss said, as if it happened every day. Then he strode away. So someone had cooked a stew, or the woman at the farm had sent up a pot. We would all sit and eat until it was gone, dipping ends of baguettes into gravy and finishing off with Serge's coffee. What he put into that chipped enamel coffee pot smelled vile, and we never saw any beans or grinder in the cabin, just a battered tin full of pungent black powder. At least we had plenty of sugar.

Eric and I hurried with axes thrown over opposite shoulders.

'What about her?' I asked.

He knew who I meant. 'What about her? The strength of a stevedore, she has, and the eyes of an angel. She presses the books. She piles them into crates. When the printer comes back for them, she has them wrapped in brown paper, tied with binding twine. She knots her hands behind her back, you know? Bold – like she expects praise. Never lowered her eyes in her life.'

The others had started on the stew, and we did our best with broken bits of bread and twisted spoons. Some smoked between mouthfuls. There were waves of silence and gobbled speech, and body warmth from work started to dissipate into the freezing night, against which we swore and hunched our backs.

I ate bits of carrot and potato in gravy; bits of unidentifiable meat and turnip greens, and thought of Colmar: thought of the girl with boy's hair in the bookbinder's shop. Thought of books. Eric had his head bent over a dented bowl that steamed slightly. His hand shook: the hand with the blackened thumb. The man was cold. What was he doing there, I wondered. No books, nothing to read. He told me once he wrote poems and stories; he read authors whose names he rattled off as if he were mentioning family names.

8

The morning had us cutting logs. We cut beams for the new barn, which was to stand on the rise above the camp. I could imagine it, black and solid against the sky, bigger than any barn I ever saw. Serge wanted it for goats. He had seen the woman at the farm strain huge cheeses in cloth, and when they were hung, they dripped their whey, smelling salty: smelling of abundance. I imagined milking goats, looking into their slits of eyes, handling them by bent horns. Now, goats and woodworking were replaced in my mind by a girl with a boy's head. A girl I had never seen, with arms to strangle a bull. Shoulders like a boy. I smelled glue and heard the crackle of thick paper when my twisted boots crunched the frozen ground on the path we cut to the road. I cut beams. I cut joists and struts and thought of short hair and powerful shoulders; hair like that of urchins who watched us when we took our unwashed bodies and unshaven faces to the baths.

I lay awake and planned. In a fortnight, I was on the train to Colmar. Without a word to Eric or giving notice to Serge, I tramped my way through the backstretch past the woman's farm. I looked through low branches at the village lights, where the redhead sold pastis and the scrooge at the baths counted francs, and then I turned toward the railway, knowing where I was heading, but not why.

I cannot remember getting off the train at Colmar. I only recall lights on the main street and my reflection in darkened shopwindows. I finally sat on a bench on the forecourt of a church with a broken gargoyle. When it got light, I would look for the bookbinder's shop, I thought. But late yellow light that stained the church steps and woke me revealed an audience of children staring at my old boots, scarred hands and hatless head. I was unshaven, dirty and stiff.

Their accent was rounded and loose, they did not smile. A girl pointed to a café where a man in a white apron stood on a clean threshold as if he expected me. His coffee was hot, sweet and as good as Serge's was vile. He sat opposite me at an iron table and silently poured me coffee after coffee until the pot was drained.

'I am looking for the bookbinder.'

'Henri Nener.'

That told me nothing about the man or the location of his shop.

'He will have no work for you.' The cafe owner stood and reached behind him for a large biscuit. He placed it in front of me. Its scent was the scent of warm kitchens and aniseed. Then he told me where the bindery was.

Before I left, I gave him the first coins of Serge's wages I ever spent, except for the occasional shower and pastis in the village.

She was standing in the doorway. I tried to look only at her eyes. She was lean, leaner than we all got in the war.

'I'm here to see your husband.' What could I say? It was the first thing that came to my head, so I said it.

She threw back her head and the laugh rang on old rafters behind her. 'That's very difficult, seeing I have none!' She laughed again and her eyes were the colour of river mud.

'Your employer, then.' My confusion was total. I started away.

'Don't go.' She spoke gently, as if to a child. 'If you are looking for the bookbinder, he'll be here presently. Sit by the stove.' She reached for a three-legged stool and I saw her powerful forearms and square shoulders.

'Monsieur,' she said, looking straight into my eyes, 'he'll see to your business when he comes. I must work.'

With her back to me, she counted sheets of printed paper and I studied her. The hair was not as short as I expected. It grew in light wisps past her high collar; light curls lacing her neck and face. The colour of new wood. She had a black leather apron bound tightly round the smallest waist I ever saw.

Her trousers were baggy, rolled nearly to her knees. I looked for the presses. They were lined up at the far end of the long room: a huge one with a red handle and

11

seven or eight smaller ones. They held books in a tight horizontal clench.

Fig. 3.--Simple Press.

It was then I noticed the smell. Centuries of the same stench in one breath. I gagged. My stomach turned.

'It's boiling.' She mumbled to herself and wiped her hand on the seat of her pants. With two large quilted wads, she removed the pot from the stove and rested it on a trivet. It was incredible: she seemed inured to the horrible smell that rose and engulfed her. I stared. A hand still gripped the pot handle. With the other, she stirred.

My disbelief held me as she stood in the smell, stirring glue. I stumbled and leaned outside, my stomach and the morning's coffee heaving. It was the smell of hell. I bent over and retched – and spied the worn but polished shoes of the bookbinder. He watched me as I straightened and collected my wits.

I gulped huge draughts of air and tried to address the small man. 'Monsieur...'

'It is only the glue smell.' His voice was pleasant and serene. 'Please – sit out here. It's better for those not used to it. Camille!' He called for her from the door. 'Fetch this man a glass of wine. He is quite overcome.' He seemed amused.

It was some time before I was able to study him. He came out into the sunshine to see whether I was sufficiently recovered, wearing an apron identical to the girl's black one. His hands were clasped gracefully. They were strong hands, but embodying a certain expression and softness: like women's hands, with oval nails neatly trimmed. His thumbs crossed each other like a saint's. 'You want work?' he asked, quite pleasantly. 'I cannot offer you work right now. Camille does a lot. Camille does almost everything.' His face was impassive.

I looked up. He faced the street from the doorway, standing in the sun, apron clean and gleaming, small head steady on wrinkled neck. A small pair of rimless glasses perched on his forehead. He looked away.

Camille was in the doorway. 'Quatre-vingts huit pages,' she said in a soft voice.

He gave her slow, clipped instructions and she re-entered. There was placidity in their exchange that spoke of a quiet intimacy. She rustled paper inside. I heard the clang of the glue-pot, and felt ill once more.

When I caught my breath, I spoke to him again. 'Eric told me about your business,' I managed.

'Eric!' he exclaimed. 'Where is Eric? From where have you come? Do you travel great distances to tell me of my brother?'

I could not decipher his expression. Was he angry? Happy?

'How is Eric?' His hands unclasped and I thought he would grasp my shoulder. Instead, he touched the doorjamb and sat unsteadily on the threshold.

I hesitated. The man had no idea, then, that his brother lived in a forest camp, barely eighty-five kilometres away, employed by a stern man with vague dreams of a goat farm, of a cheese dairy, of a barn as big as a railway station. He had no idea of the cold, the sparse coarse food, the futility of washing. He did not know of what lay outside Belfort: the draughty shed, the woman's farm and the bay mares.

Perhaps I should not tell him his brother was a mere half dozen railway stations away. 'I come from Neufchateau.' I lied quickly, thinking of the furthest town I could of which I had a vague knowledge. 'I was in a linen factory there.'

He tilted his head. 'With those hands?'

I looked at my calloused palms and saw my mistake. 'Uh – I spent the last three weeks clearing some fields for a Belgian farmer.' That at least was the truth, but I did not have to say where the Belgian farmer had his farm.

'And Eric?'

'He is well. Ah – tired and cold like the rest of us, but well enough.'

He nodded. 'Good. He left suddenly.' He saw the need for some explanation. 'We fought. I regret some words ...' Contrition showed in his gentle hands. They clasped as if in prayer. 'I was hasty.' He paused. Unwilling to confide in a total stranger, he turned to more practical things. 'You will have a bed,' he said hospitably. 'Food. You must rest. Neufchateau is miles away. You must have had a hard journey. It is cold on the train.' Then he looked away.

The girl was in the door again. She held up four fingers. 'And four others in two hours. I can turn the first ones out now. No need –' She held up a hand when he stood up. 'No – sit. I can turn them on my own.'

After he had looked at the presses, he took me to a small house in a shady lane where all the doors were painted green. He opened a door and led me to a small room like a pantry behind the kitchen. On a platter, he placed a small peppered cheese, an end of sausage and a whole loaf. There was a sharp knife hanging by a leather thong on a nail. He put it on the platter also. 'After this,' he said, as if giving me some work instructions, 'climb to the last bedroom on the right upstairs and sleep. It is your room until you decide to leave.'

I could not express my gratitude gracefully, so I said nothing, and nodded.

I heard them downstairs, moving about softly not to disturb me. I had slept under a thick quilt for over seven hours. I went down and saw him bent over the stove, stirring something fragrant in a wide pan. 'Sit, sit.' He looked me up and down. 'I hope you have rested well.'

'I did not realise how tired I was,' I said apologetically.

He smiled. 'My daughter will bring you wine.' His daughter! This was Eric's niece. I remembered his rough hands circling a phantom waist, his clipped words of accurate description. His eyes were slits and his stained fingers had straightened my cigarettes as he spoke of her.

She had to touch my shoulder to make me see she held a glass in front of me. She leaned across and said, 'Here.' She gave me ruby red wine in a thick tumbler.

I was at their house three days before he asked me if I thought I could stand the smell of glue in the shop. 'We have started re-binding the parish records. It is a big job. We do not have the Grammère to help any more. We could do with your help, after all, with undoing the old bindings – if you can stand the air.'

'I can hardly refuse after your magnificent hospitality,' I said candidly. 'You have not taken payment. I ...'

'I offer to you what I should have given to Eric. A lost brother ... perhaps a gained friend.' His contrite expression filled me with guilt. I eyed his daughter surreptitiously at every evening meal; wished her into my bed each night. My body leaned involuntarily towards hers. I was perhaps filling the very place from where he had angrily expelled Eric. But Eric was her uncle. It was hard to think of Eric, the man with rough hands and blackened thumb, as anyone's uncle. Eric and his axe in the forest: straightening a damp cigarette on a filthy trouser knee. Eric: downing a quick glass of pastis and teasing me about my lusty examination of the redhead in the village. Eric: scraping bark off a huge trunk and sniffing at Serge's plans for a cheese factory. Eric: who described to me the shape of his niece's body.

Eric's brother, Henri, expected an answer, and looked at me querulously.

'I will work as hard as I can,' I promised.

The stench in the shop was hard to stomach, especially when they boiled up the glue and stirred it. Both totally inured, they dipped hogs hair brushes into the mess and neatly, like artists, painted sticky brown lines on the stitched spines of books. They handled thin calf leather like precious fabric, stretching it between four hands, working in silent cooperation.

I sat out on the sunlit bench for most of the first few days, unpicking old twine from the backs of ancient

17

registers. I had to be careful not to damage the script or crease the parchment. The girl was hardly aware of my presence. She did not see me watch her when she turned the spalancated arms of the book presses. Her strength was formidable for a woman her size. Then she handled small tools with intricate care and grace.

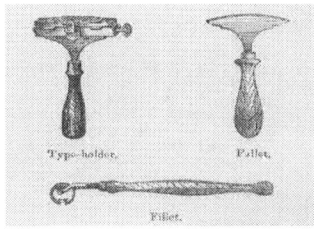

Ignorant of her ability, anyone who saw her on the street would consider her a waif, a mere slip of a girl.

She scarcely knew I was there. Part of me enjoyed my invisibility. Part of me wanted her to notice me. I had changed. I was clean. Regular baths and a haircut saw to most of the superficial neglect of the forest. Soon my callused hands lost their abrasiveness, my cheeks filled out, and I stopped hunching my shoulders from the cold.

I looked at myself in their mirror on the stairs and saw that, in new clothes and nourished skin, I looked more like who I was than when I had arrived.

'Walter,' they called me. 'Walter!' they used my name as if I were a family member. These days I heard my name more often than ever before. I responded, sometimes in wonder at my good fortune. Weeks passed.

When we were working on the notary's registers, I realised I did not notice the glue smell any more. I looked up from counting pages and saw Camille stirring the glue pot vigorously, adding more pellets from the sack.

Her smile was warm and intimate, not unlike the ones she reserved for her father. 'You nearly threw up, that first day you came from Neufchateau, remember?'

I still felt guilty about having lied about my previous whereabouts. I lowered my head to appear embarrassed about my weak stomach. Really, I was pleased she noticed anything about me. That evening, we all joked about me getting used to the smell. She put a hand on mine on the table, in full view of her father. His expression stayed as calm as before.

I slept little that night. My thoughts were full of foolish hope and schemes. 'Walter,' she called me: Walter the bookbinder.

When I took her to the local fair, she wore a dress. I had never seen her in a dress. It was light green, incongruous with her short brown hair, but the velvet sash circled her small waist tightly and I could hardly contain myself as she took my arm. Next time we are alone together, I promised myself, I would attempt a kiss. I would kiss her mouth as I had imagined so many times, and the eyes the colour of river mud would close and she would kiss me back.

We bound all the notary's books and there was little to do for days. Then we started on some library books someone brought in a van from Langres. The shop was stacked with them. We all worked hard in silence, exiled from everyone by the smell of the shop. And in the middle of the order, when we were counting how many we did and how many remained, a man stood in the doorway.

'Eric!' Henri's voice sounded strangled and unusually harsh.

Eric: I hardly recognised him, because I had forgotten the dirt, the scratches and what a fortnight's growth of beard could do to a man's appearance.

More strangely, he did not recognise me. I said something and he started and looked again.

'You!' He spat. 'You left without a word.' His eyes were slits and resentment garbled his words. 'Since then ... I don't know what I thought ... You left without a word – I thought you were a friend.'

'Your brother was very good to me.' I looked at Henri, who stood shock still in the middle of his foul-smelling shop.

'You are welcome, as you have always been welcome.' He spoke to Eric softly, as if he had recovered his composure, but I could see he was unnerved. His eyes went to his daughter. She turned silently to the glue pot.

'You kicked me out.' Eric addressed his brother slowly. 'And I have come back.' He paused. 'I really don't know why ... but I have come back.'

The thoughts that raced through my head were interrupted by his quizzing look. He was forming questions, looking from me to Camille. He could always tell what I was thinking, so I could not let him see my eyes.

'I have come from far away,' he said.

Why did he lie? My ruse of Neufchateau was sure to be discovered and I would seem a liar in Camille's eyes. I resigned myself to failure where I stood, even when Henri hurried him away to the house where I spent so many hopeful nights. How was I to explain why I had come to his brother's, when I did not know the reason myself? Was it that I wanted so badly to see the hair and waist and boy's shoulders he had described? How was I to explain that to him, her uncle?

How was he to deny his own perverse desire of her? I looked at the girl. She did not flinch to be found staring at me.

21

She shrugged. 'They have always quarrelled,' she said. 'He won't be here long. Did he work for the Belgian farmer too?'

I nodded. Well, he had.

'I will kill you.' His voice rumbled as we passed each other that night. 'I will kill you if I find you even touched her hand or her shoulder.' His gnarled thumb was reflected in the mirror. 'I say a few words, and you run like a thief in the night. Here. Of all places, here.' Then he looked apologetic, crushed. When he looked up again, his eyes glimmered. 'I'm sorry, Walter. I'm sorry. But I will. I'll kill you with my axe if you so much as look at her in lust.'

From then on, he was as friendly as at Serge's camp. We worked in the bindery with his brother and his niece; the four of us absorbed in books, enveloped by the stench and surrounded by tools and implements of the trade. We handled tanned and dyed skins and carefully folded linen for the covers. We cut board and twine and threaded long sharp awls. We wielded brushes heavy with the glue whose thick odour lay in the air, in our nostrils and in our lungs. We smelled of it.

We worked for days without a break, finishing a large order from Dijon. I would look across the shop at

Eric, taking in the visible improvement good food and long rest made on his frame.

His eyes were another matter. They were now thin slits, his feigned friendliness like a threat, like a stench that surrounded him. When he addressed the girl, his words sprayed and hissed ingratiatingly between his teeth.

I could see her cringe. He thumbed pages with his bent blackened nail, turning his head to watch her as she worked, as she stooped gracefully to pick up a stack of paper.

Things shifted. I do not remember exactly when I realised Camille was looking at me across the shop as I worked. She also looked at me across the dinner table at night, or when I stood outside for a smoke. Much to my frustration, she walked past me in my corner when she could take a shorter way to the stove. She smiled and made conversation I would have been overjoyed to continue if it were not for Eric. Desire and fear rolled together like belches of fumes from the glue pot. I could no longer enjoy my warming towards her, the irrepressible reactions of my body as I heard her pass my room in the night.

Eric would shift audibly in his bed, and I would lie awake in trepidation, stifling desire as if it were a newborn kitten.

'You are even less talkative than when you first arrived.' Henri Nener was genial, seating me next to his daughter and pouring wine. Could it be he did not see the venom in his brother's eyes?

'You should have seen him drinking pastis and conversing with a certain redhead!' Eric laughed, and placed his hand for a brief moment on his niece's.

There was an almost audible crackle, a flash from Henri's eyes. The hand retreated quickly, but the atmosphere remained charged with rage, with confusion. The brothers were caught in inexpressible battle, while I could not look at Camille's eyes without discomfort. Would she believe what Eric said about the redhead? I longed to look at her, to register in gestures, if not in speech, what I was afraid to say. But Eric looked at her first. She smiled at me and turned away to cut bread. I could not decide if his looks were malevolent or crazily calm, but I saw the axe under his bed, saw him fingering the sharp knife hanging by its thong in the pantry, and could not sleep peacefully at night if he saw me accept her friendliness.

Her friendliness? I did not know what it was any more. She started to send puzzled smiles at me across the shop. She must have wondered why I was no longer eager to sit next to her at table. Did I remember our knees touching?

Fingering a length of beautifully dyed and tooled green calfskin together, I avoided her fingers, I avoided her looks and I avoided Eric's, confounded and crazed by my position. I sat out on the bench as I had when the smell would make me sick.

My hands became soft and sensitive. I felt the beauty of the leather, remembered how her own hands were: powerful yet soft. And her father's hands, with crossed thumbs like a church statue's. And Eric's hands were there now, still coarse from the forest: the forest of which neither of us spoke. Everything became strained, complicated. Eric made his intentions quite plain to me – yet could hardly show them to his brother, who threw him out once before for daring to admit to an attraction to Camille.

'Look at that waist,' he hissed once, when we were loading books into a van. Camille folded brown paper, for a moment unaware of his sly gaze. She looked up and caught us both looking at her.

Her father stopped winding twine onto a spool. 'It's time we all stopped for the day,' he said vaguely. His confusion and sadness were too strong to bear.

'That girl could go on for ever!' Eric's clumsily hidden lewdness filled the space between us like a threat.

That evening, near the pantry, I found words. 'What has got into you, Eric? You used to talk about books.

Your talk was all of authors, of poetry.' He was hardly the man I remembered in the forest.

'And now,' he rumbled sarcastically, 'I seem more familiar with an axe. I am more comfortable with something sharp in my hands!' He spat the last words as I dove quickly out of the low doorway. His bent thumb caressed the honed knife.

I left as quietly as I arrived. A bigger bag, a heavier heart. The train rumbled in from stations on the border and Belfort, where I had laboured in the forest with Eric and Serge and a host of other faceless and nameless war-scarred men. It drew to a slow stop and I looked round to a movement behind the shelter. It was Eric.

'Walter,' he called. He had not said my name more than a couple of times the entire time I stayed at his brother's.

I stopped with my hand on the train handrail, speechless.

'You do well to leave.' His eyes were blank.

I could not find an answer, and lifted both my feet onto the step.

'It is useless, with my brother ...' He rambled on, as if he had not seen I was leaving. I knew what he meant.

'She is headstrong, like –' The train whistle cut off his sentence.

'Adieu.' It was all I could manage. I did not want to talk to him. Again, I was leaving like a thief in the night.

When I reached Neufchateau I looked for a church and sat on its front steps until a gendarme appeared in the morning bustle around the shops. Perhaps I should look for work. Perhaps I could survive on what I saved until I decided where to go and what to do. I left my suitcase with the owner of a delicatessen and wandered about the town.

'No, there is no bookbinder near here.' The newsagent looked up from his counter and his paper folding when I asked. He looked curious but I did not say anything else.

It seemed I would not be able to use my experience in Neufchateau, but I stayed for countless idle weeks that passed, as strangers do at a station. Looking in the paper for work was more like a pastime than a useful undertaking. There was no forest clearing or book binding to be done.

I went along to a tannery once, to inquire for work and found the stench not overpowering, but too similar to what I was used to. It caught at my throat.

Then I saw it: a small advertisement. Wanted: bookbinder for large job. Apply – La Petite Brocheuse in Dinant.

I was on the train that evening, thinking it could be the church wanting its registers bound, or the local library with volumes of local history. I gave no thought to materials or tools. With none of my own, how was I to take on a bookbinding assignment, even though I now knew something of how to fulfil the task? I sat back and decided to cross that bridge when I came to it.

The train was an old one, shuddering along to its destination and mine reluctantly. I arrived in a strong breeze, the kind that precedes a storm. There was no such place as La Petite Brocheuse in Dinant. The town outside the station was quiet, deserted, with street lamps spraying pools of grey light in the rain that heralded my arrival. But Dinant is no different to Neufchateau, or any other place on the whole continent, if you are alone.

The only boarding house that looked affordable was called *Jenny Lind*. I took a room for a week. What difference did anything make? Perhaps I could find farming work on the outskirts. I hardly knew where I was.

'Belgium is divided into two,' said the guesthouse owner sagely, tapping his pipe and turning the book for me to sign. 'Half is like this and half like that.' He rolled his heavy hand over, and over again, no doubt in some political meaning. I cared little. He spoke French and nothing else.

'Not even English,' he insisted, grinning.

In the morning, he served me croissants, coffee and the same conversation, which had to be one-sided as I found I had little time for him.

'Are you sure there is no place called La Petite Brocheuse anywhere near here?' I was becoming angry about coming all the way for nothing. 'Is there no bookbinder in town?'

'A bookbinder? You are looking for a bookbinder? There is one at the foot of the steep street behind the church.'

The familiar smell of glue greeted me at the doorway. I peered into darkness and saw a young man with glasses, who was sewing pages together.

'Bonjour!' he shouted merrily in welcome. His voice boomed through the smell and I looked for the glue pot. It was a small affair perched on a paraffin stove on a counter near a splattered wall.

'Did you put the notice in the Neufchateau newspaper?' I asked immediately. I had lost all interest in pleasantries.

There was silence, and then his voice boomed back. 'No! What notice?' He seemed a jovial fellow. He came to the front part of the room, which was stacked with torn books, sheaves of paper and bundles of skin and linen. 'Neufchateau? What are you talking about?' He had a wide smile and dancing eyes behind thick lenses, which magnified the blue colour ten-fold. A shock of hair stood out in the middle of a balding skull. He kept flattening it. The brilliant eyes gave him a deceptively youthful appearance. He was much older than he seemed.

'There was an advert about a bookbinding position,' I explained. 'I thought it must have been you. Is this place La Petite Brocheuse?'

'Ha ha!' He burst into peals of laughter that seemed to set everything a-shake.

Behind him, just in my line of sight, a leather curtain at the back of the room ballooned in a draught. A boy appeared, pushing the curtain before him.

'It was me.' It was her. Camille stood in the middle of the jumbled mess, holding an awl and a ball of twine. She looked like a boy.

'Camille!'

'Walter!' Her smile was bright. Her hair was shorter than I ever saw it.

'This is La Petite Brocheuse!' shouted the bookbinder in glee. 'She appeared out of the blue one day and said she could bind books. She was right!' He boomed another laugh at the ceiling. 'Now you! There are bookbinders coming out of every corner!'

Camille and I stared at each other. 'Why are you here?' I asked, mystified. I needed to know why she had left the bindery in France, coming all the way into Belgium. It could not have been easy to leave her father.

'Perhaps you know why.' Her reply was quiet. She shrugged and said no more.

'You two want to talk.' The bookbinder smiled when he said the obvious words. 'But get out of this smell!' He exclaimed and looked at me. 'It must be killing you.'

'I'm used to it,' I said.

'Yes, and much worse.' Her smile was brilliant.

Her eyes left mine only once when we sat at the small café, during her breathless account of what happened in Colmar after my departure. Her whole body shrank at Eric's name.

She looked into her cup. 'He became incoherent, you see. He ... he went to great lengths to be alone with me. It only happened once – but that was enough.' She looked up then.

I controlled my anger, but disgust was plain on my face. 'What did he do?' I asked.

'I ... Nothing. He did nothing.' Her cheeks reddened; she took her hands from the table and placed them in her lap, a deceptively soft feminine movement. 'He tried – he clasped my waist from behind, dug his chin in my shoulder, that's all.'

I uttered a grunt, looked around, attempting to hide my disgust. 'I would have –'

'I know.' Then she smiled wryly, but only for an instant. 'I did.'

'What, you? Hit him?'

'I had to! I moved quickly, shook free and twisted one of his arms back, turning it – like the screw on the press.' Her eyes clouded with shame.

My own eyes were wide, incredulous, but why was I surprised? I had seen her lift huge bundles, load stacks of books onto a barrow. Her arms were as strong as mine.

'Then?' I asked.

'Then I threatened him, slowly and softly – but viciously. Threatened him with anything I could think of. He was gone within hours. I was miserable. For some reason I was miserable.'

Her eyes filled with tears, unshed. 'I got on a night train like you did. My father – I think he understood. But I had no idea where you went or where to go myself.'

'Where I went?' I breathed.

She nodded. 'I found myself in Belgium after catching train after train after train. This was the first place after my money finished where I could find a job.' Her eyes were the colour of chestnuts.

'And the advertisement?'

Her hands clasped mine on the table. 'I had to find you. I tried to remember all the places you mentioned and placed notices in the papers of each town.' She tilted her head, pleading for understanding. 'What else could I do?' Her words were soft, but they told of valiant efforts to find me. To find me.

'I never expected to see you again,' I said. It was the truth.

Camille smiled. 'You give up so easily. I have to be headstrong enough for both of us.' Somehow, forgiveness was woven into the accusation. 'You left without a word.'

I remembered the identical words spat from a thin contemptuous mouth.

I never saw Eric again, but there are nights I dream of a forest where a chainsaw buzzes and horses crash through undergrowth dragging chained logs. He sits on a felled tree tapping a cigarette on a dirty trouser knee, talking about a woman with a waist the size of his circled hands. I dream of places where the only smell is of pine needles crushed underfoot, where the scarce water is not for washing and the food is sparse and Spartan. I dream of goats I never saw and a barn I never built.

Now, I wake to the stench of glue from the bones of old horses, bubbling in a small pot over a kerosene stove in the shop below, and drink good coffee poured from a small red enamel pot. I turn when I hear hot water streaming into a basin, which means she is going to wash her hair.

After Agnes

The house is gone,' he said. 'All I can do now is try to remember it.'

Although I sat in a cane armchair across from him and could easily hear what he said, I leaned forward and Saul Koolhoven bent toward me.

So we were caught, the two of us so different, in a halo of light from his porch lamp: the cabin lamp from a trawler.

His skin looked like gilded parchment. His hands were folded, like in a grotesque prayer. Arthritis had gnarled his fingers and they were splayed and angled so he had limited movement and could hardly grip a thing. His knees, too, had been affected. He sat with them wide apart, sometimes creaking them together carefully, lower lip between his teeth. 'You see, she waited years – saved for years, salting away the money without my knowing. Ah, how clever, how clever she was.' He shook his head in what I took to be a mixture of admiration and regret: then he leaned his head against the cushioned cane of the only chair he found comfortable.

He was telling me of his life with Agnes – whose niece I was – their stilted but strangely companionable relationship that lasted the last fifteen years before her death.

'Come, I'll show you,' he wheezed as he rose. It was the first time his accent was detectable. Until that moment, he had none. I could imagine his young voice, before his racked body had rasped it with its contortions. He shuffled ahead of me, bent knees and rounded back held with a superb effort to convey an illusion of uprightness. But it gave way occasionally, so he submitted to a limp, a monstrous genuflection, as if he knelt at the altar of twisted bones.

'This is what she built instead.' The Dutch intonation and soft consonants were strong now. His hand swept a semi-circle in front of us. It was a modern lounge, with a dining room in the el. The walls were covered with paintings.

Agnes had been a collector of some note, travelling Europe to find exactly what she happened to be after at the time. I paused in an attempt to calculate mentally the riches she accumulated by her acumen.

'Fantastic.' I was impressed.

'Oh yes, she had an eye,' he said, knowing my thoughts. 'I'll never be at a loss financially. Sometimes all I do is lend them the blessed things!' He pointed at a pair of landscapes, smiled, shook his head and grunted, perhaps in pain.

'This is the kitchen,' he said, without need. The well-lit space was bright with steel and black laminated surfaces. 'All I can do now is remember the old wood range, the huge lamp we had, hanging over the refectory table. I remember the monks who sold it to us – that large slab of a table, scored and scarred by a million knives over centuries. One corner had a worn hollow where bread was cut – bread for a century of monastery life, cut by a knife that dug its own impression into a corner of our table. Our table – I can only just remember it now.'

I found it hard to do anything but nod to acknowledge his talking. He needed no spurring to go on. He opened a door, caught on the end of one of his jerky limps, leaning on the knob in a dramatic pose. I knew not to help him. One of his legs shuddered.

Looking through the door and down a steep flight of wooden steps, I saw tier upon tier of bottles, lying on their sides. It was dimly lit, ordered, damp and quiet.

'She always kept a good cellar. I can't go down now. Could you...?'

I was halfway down before he said the next word. My inquiring look made him rattle off wine names. He pointed with a grotesque gnarled finger here and there, until I was clutching half a dozen dusty bottles to my chest.

'You'll also have to uncork one, I'm afraid,' he grimaced, and looked at his hands as he turned them palms upward. The hollows created by twisted fingers were creased, permanently bowled as if to accept water. Back on his veranda, he creaked into the cane chair, which was upholstered to fit the contortions of his body.

I found a corkscrew and opened the bottle he indicated.

'Let it breathe!' he cried, happily expectant of its savouring.

I went to the kitchen and found some cheese, which I cut into small cubes, then wondered if he would be able to carry them to his mouth with such hands, so I provided a fork.

'So clever, so clever,' he mumbled when I returned.

I knew he meant Agnes, his wife Agnes, my aunt Agnes.

'I was away for weeks at a time. Shipboard life, you know. I loved it. The last tour I was able to do was – of all things – a rig shift. Hah! After all those years of working as First Engineer on tankers, I was reduced to bumping along the oceans on a square rig. Oceans! I have sailed oceans, taking all sorts of cargoes to all sorts of ports. And I know ports. I knew people everywhere, and yes, I suppose...' He paused to gauge my expression.

I nodded slightly, meaning he would not have to censor his reminiscing.

'Yes, I suppose, I strayed and erred a few times as sailors do, but nothing dramatic. Nothing strong enough to overpower her ability to ... She was powerful, you see. Power, love – I don't know what it was.' He shifted in the chair, trying to grasp his knees and failing, rubbing a finger across the top of his hand.

I passed him a goblet of red wine, realising the minute I did he could not possibly hold its stem. I quickly tipped the contents into a thick tumbler from the sideboard, bringing it to him and placing it in his grasp as he nodded thankfully, eyes hooded.

'Always, she'd greet me with announcements about changes she made, so even on the way home from the port I'd know there was new carpet, different curtains, the study moved to upstairs ... or whatever. She was continually changing things, buying different clothes for herself, papering the walls in odd colours – and later paintings, always buying paintings.'

'Did you –' I started, not wanting to puncture the night with my voice. Although he needed no urging to talk, I wanted him to feel it was a conversation of some sort. Monosyllables and small exclamations on my part were all that was needed.

'I had no idea she was saving any money. I never questioned what she did with it all, anyway. We lived well. We entertained. When I was land bound – that's what she called it. Saul is land bound, she would say. When I was at home, we had friends around a lot. We went to the theatre, to the mountains. She could ski, you see. We went where she wanted. We went to galleries in Paris – and Antwerp. She liked the Jewish quarter there. We bought jewellery. We bought clothes. I never thought she'd salt away enough to ... but she did!' His exclamation was half-angry, and half filled with a kind of admiration for his dead wife's deception. He shook his head. 'All I can do now is remember the old house. The rounded staircase with the wrought iron balustrade she once painted black. The old newel post was thick, spiralled, carved in places with vine leaves and things ... there was a small window in the landing, so one could spy on visitors before coming down the stairs. That landing!' He shook his head.

'Was it…?' I started to ask a question.

He nodded and went on. 'It had two doors, one to our bedroom and the other to the Long Room, we called it.' He sipped, nodding at the taste, clamping his lips together in a tight line. 'In our bedroom she hung two pairs of yellow damask curtains on gilded pelmets. One pair hid a window and the other the door to a wooden enclosed balcony overlooking the street. A balcony of Middle Eastern style, it was, with long windows that flapped up and outward, held open by long metal-hinged hooks. Hard to describe, really. The bedroom floor was yellow and I think the furniture mahogany. Once, I returned from Reykjavik to find a new suite.'

'New?'

'New. No mahogany, no yellow damask – it was all gone, replaced with ivory lacquer and blue satin. Very chic, she said. Striped elegant wallpaper. Ages ago.'

I rose from my cane chair which, unlike his, was unpadded and becoming rather uncomfortable and cold. He took it as a prompt, and we moved to the lounge. I carried in his special chair at his bidding, and set it near the fire. He carefully closed the double doors behind us, struggling with the catch. I did not help him. He finally managed to get his fingers round the handle and turned it quickly, then reached and drew the curtains tightly. Without talking, he walked in his uneven gait to the electric fire and switched it on with his thumb.

I pointed to it and smiled, somehow knowing what would ensue.

'We used to have an open fireplace you could walk into. Well – I could walk into it now,' he laughed. 'I'd always leave enough split logs for her to burn in my

41

absences. It was one thing I could do for her, cut wood. Everything else she had under absolute control. She was never in any bother. But that fireplace ...' he sighed. 'It blasted huge belches of hot air all over the lower storey. We sat in it and revelled. She sat in her red chair on one side, like that, looking at art catalogues. I sat opposite her, like this. Why don't you knit or something, I'd say, and she'd shrug as if to say clothes were easy enough to buy ready-made.' He looked at me pointedly. 'Do you knit?'

'A bit.'

'I'd have loved her to make me a thick jumper to take away to sea. Some of the men, even the able bodies, had home-knitted sweaters with cables on them. Clever designs. Hours of knitting by their wives on land, you know.'

As I poured wine into the thick tumbler held in the gnarled fist, I wondered whether I should make him one. He looked at the electric fire and then at me. I followed his gaze and saw a neatly folded knee rug on an armchair. I placed it in his bent lap. His knees were wide apart and he winced as he drew them together and swept the rug quickly over them. He ran a hand over his full head of grey hair, then down his thin face.

'Are you tired yet?' I asked, moving closer to the fire.

He did not answer. He closed his eyes and I studied his face closely. His skin was not as creased as I thought.

A few lines etched by pain drew around his mouth, and some etched by the weather folded around his eyes, but his chin and cheeks were healthy and tanned, as smooth as his hands were crooked.

He started to talk again. 'Once, she met me off the ship and drove us to a hotel. I thought it was a surprise, a kind of romantic interlude she planned after a long absence. I remember it was the time I worked two tours of duty end to end, replacing an engineer who lost a leg. Squashed between two ships, he was. Anyway, we went to a hotel. That night, she explained there was nowhere else for us to stay. Nowhere else, I exclaimed. What happened to the house? She said only one word – demolished. I could not believe it. It was the only real big argument we ever had.' He paused.

'Really?'

'No – there was another, of course. Anyway, she was patient with me and my goings and comings, and I could easily tolerate her ways because I knew I'd soon sail away. That's how it is with men like me. We can put up with anything because we know it's not for long. Even women like Agnes. She had that energy, that draining spirit, that restlessness. She'd have done well to have a seagoing career herself!' He laughed.

I said something, and he nodded.

'Where was I? Ah – like I said. It was one of the most serious disagreements we ever had, about something

43

that could never be reversed. Never. She had the house pulled down. She was building a new one. A new one, imagine that.' He raised both hands to shoulder height to stress his dismay; lowered them together with a wince. His fingers twitched.

'What...?' I started.

He did not let me finish. 'I was never so disappointed in my life. I mean ... we had disappointments, understand. When we discovered she couldn't have children – that's a long story. Then my brother tried to seduce her. And my own escapades, of course, or the ones she discovered. Well, like I say, we had disappointments and troubles, but nothing as irreversible as the house. Now, I can do nothing but remember it. And the way I kept looking at her, all the while we stayed at the damned hotel. I wanted my red chair, my books. All in storage, she said. Even my models of ships.' He looked at his hands.

I looked at his hands.

He looked at me. 'Before this got bad, you see, I made a wooden model of every ship I had been on, even the ugly crates they call container ships, even the tankers. I have them all, upstairs. Come.'

We made a slow ascent up the wide modern staircase. He leaned heavily on the wide stone balustrade, and shuffled on the deep carpet. Still, he seemed able to manage stairs. What was so different about the cellar ones? The landing was set out like a gallery: model ships on shelves in three tiers. Hanging between them was memorabilia amassed during his life at sea. Lifebelts, links from chains, assorted instruments among which I could only identify a sextant, and other naval paraphernalia neatly displayed in rows. So he too had a penchant for collecting.

I gazed on the ships and at his back as he tried to walk steadily along the rows; occasionally making the jerky genuflection his arthritic knees forced him into, as if to revere the ships that had carried him all over the world.

'My ships,' he said proudly. 'In the other house they were displayed in the Long Room. We have no long room now.' He threw open a door to reveal a tidy spare bedroom. 'We have four of these. All alike, more or less.

45

And two bathrooms, one with a supposed naval theme. Nautical, I think she called it. Anchors and things, you know. It was sweet in a way. But all I can do now is remember the old one. In the old house, the bath was iron, with ball and claw feet. The gas water heater was so temperamental we always left the door open for air – or a quick getaway! Always too hot, that heater. I remember lying in the bath wondering whether the thing would blow up over my head and fill me with shrapnel. She would lean over and wash her hair in the basin and shout out to me, always too hot!' He laughed, as one would at a child.

'In summer,' he went on, wanting to fill in all the detail of memory, 'the opaque glass of the tiny window was very warm, so a lizard would come and rest on it, every year, until ... I never saw it again.'

Back downstairs, I poured him more wine. 'Shall I uncork a couple for you before I go?'

'Yes, and push the cork in part of the way so I can pull it out with my teeth.' He smiled and displayed them, tapping a gold bottom one. It would bring on another reminiscence.

'Knocked clean out of my head by a feisty first mate, this tooth was. Just like that, because I said Antwerp women were wonderful and he happened to have a Belgian wife. What would you know about my wife! he roared, and punched me in the mouth. I told Agnes the story and she laughed at the time. Took me to the best dentist in town. About four months later, after another trip on a different ship, she surprised me in the middle of dinner by asking how I knew what Antwerp women were like.' He shook his head. 'I knew what she meant. That winter, I was repentant and spent most of the nights in port, playing cards and chess with the skipper and writing to her.'

'Poker,' I said.

He laughed ruefully. 'Saul Koolhoven, you're rotten at poker, said that captain once, after he relieved me of most of my pay. Ha! But I'm sure Agnes preferred getting a bit less for it. Ha! She was not a jealous type but she wielded something, you know. Guile. Power. That winter, I think it was, the new house was completed. No wooden framed windows, no shutters. No floorboards, but carpet. No balcony! She showed me round on my arrival, throwing open every door and leaving lights on as we went.' His eyes misted over.

I sat back and let him ramble on.

'I was pleased to have a proper home again,' he said. 'But you know what? I had a terrific shock. Somehow, what I expected to see after those months of waiting ... was the old house.'

'But…'

'I know, I know. Reason has nothing to do with what your mind conjures after weeks at sea. She showed me round the new house and I could hardly hold back the tears because I expected to see the big wooden front door. The wrought iron balustrade, the winding stairs, my ships in the Long Room, the temperamental water heater, and the huge fireplace. I was shocked and embarrassed at the same time – and she felt something. I knew then she felt something like regret, but it was fleeting ...' He paused. His hands were trembling. He placed a bent forefinger on his forehead.

I did not know where to look.

He cocked his head and saw me pour more wine. 'I am embarrassing you,' he said finally.

'No! I am more touched than anything else. And flattered that you can tell me about it.'

'You must not think I hated what she did. It was the opposite. She did nothing to wilfully annoy me. It was just ... I don't know what it was. This was her domain, you see. My life was away from her and when I was at home, I was constantly in a state of waiting. Waiting for the sea, for the ship under my feet. The smell of oil, the shouts of the men and the feel of the gunnels under my hand. The sight of port lights from a distance. Rounding a cape ...' He tailed off and tipped what was left in his glass into his mouth.

For the first time, he reached for a piece of cheese and managed miraculously to take a cube to his mouth in a jerky motion while I held my breath.

'Her life was paintings and curtains and new varnish on the doors. She never guessed my attachment to the house because perhaps I never showed it. When the new one was finished ... well, it never seemed finished, because after every trip away she showed me what she had done, added, changed. Then she started collecting those paintings. And all paid for with what she saved from my pay packets! I had no idea how much I earned. I knew the figure, of course, but not what it could buy. I was never much use with land values. Hah! Land values,' he repeated.

'What about the garden?' I asked.

'Agnes cared little about that. A boy came in. I still have him – well, he's not a boy anymore! When I stopped going to sea, I found myself at such a loss I started to potter out there myself. A relief to Agnes. She found me in the way, I suppose, not used to having me around all the time. And funnily enough, I found her cycle of patience to be more or less four weeks! Yes, for four weeks or so she'd be just like she always was when I was home. Then she withdrew.'

'Withdrew?' I repeated.

'Mm,' he mumbled. 'Distance. Solitude is what we both needed. I missed the sea and the Long Room. I went out in the garden and stayed there until dusk, learning from books and seed catalogues and from the mowing boy. You saw the camellias? Mine. The honeysuckle? I put that in, much to his consternation. Too untidy in shape, he said. Hah! Nature is untidy, I told him. Look at the ocean! You know what he said?'

'What?'

'Never been near the sea in my life, he said. Imagine that – a whole life without being on a ship! Never swam in the sea. Never arrived at a strange port. I put that right immediately. Drove him down to the local port and had an old captain friend take him on an excursion. An education, it was. He looks at me differently now. All your life on ships, he said once. Could have been admiration or disgust, I don't know!'

'Was that before Agnes died?' I asked. 'By the way, how …?'

He did not let me finish the question. He held a hand high, gnarled fingers caught in radiation from the electric fire. 'I killed her. I killed her, you know.' His eyes were bright.

I did not know what to say. But my disbelief or silence would not stop him talking. The wine bottle was empty and he signalled almost impatiently with a twisted hand for me to uncork another. 'About three years after I retired … The pain in my hands and knees was something awful. The power in that pain … I used to think pain was female!' he laughed.

I smiled, welcoming the tinge of humour, black as it was. Did I want him to continue?

He went on regardless. 'Agnes was quite wonderful in her own way, although I found as always it was best to agree with what she wanted, even when it was my own body in question – my pain after all!' He threw his hands up again in a show of comic frustration, which had a sad effect. 'But sometimes she was impossible,' he stressed. 'And sometimes I proved impossible myself. My twisting bones. I got in the way. We couldn't travel easily any more. She felt guilty about skiing, about hopping plane to plane in search of some painting or other.'

'She travelled alone?'

'Oh, frequently! Once, she returned from four days in Antwerp with the most gorgeous diamond. I found it hard to believe we still had the money for things like that. After all, my medical bills were enormous. Anyway, we argued. She was standing in the kitchen clutching half a dozen bottles to her chest, just as you did a short while ago. Just like that. And then it happened. I killed her, you see.'

'What did you do?' The question left my lips before I could stop myself.

Saul Koolhoven twisted his neck, took a deep sigh, which shook his whole frame and looked at me squarely. 'I shouted at her. I was angry about the diamond, of all things. She shouted back. I was shaking and her face was red with rage. I thought it was rage. Suddenly, she fell

51

down the cellar steps, crashing with the wine bottles onto the concrete floor below.'

For a few moments, we were silent. I heard the ticking of a clock, which had gone unnoticed before. A car hummed on the lane outside. A slight drone came from the electric fire. Saul shook. His misshapen fists clenched the chair arms and what I thought was a tear stood in the corner of one eye. Then he went on, brushing his face with one hand as he had done before.

'I can't go down there now,' he said plaintively. 'I remember her twisted shape lying in what I thought was blood. It was of course wine, whose smell rose all around me, like vinegar. I called them – I don't know who I called. I made many phone calls. The doctor, the ambulance, the police – I don't know. Suddenly the house was full of people and a kind soul was giving me a cup of tea. I don't drink tea!' He made a frustrated noise in the back of his throat and laughed, as if to lessen his own emotion.

'And then?'

'Later – I think days later – I woke with a start, half expecting to be back in the old bedroom with the window and the balcony, you know. Anyway, I woke and remembered she was gone. I told them. I told them I killed her. The argument ... the cellar steps.' Saul looked up at me, a grimace on his face. His expression seemed to urge me to agree with him.

I could only nod.

He continued, lowering his eyes for an instant. 'Rubbish, the doctor said. De Jong – had him for years. Rubbish, he said. Agnes had a heart attack, Saul, he said. He was very calm. She probably didn't even feel the impact when she fell. She died almost immediately. Sudden heart failure, you know.' He looked at me again. 'She died before she hit the concrete floor, is what he meant.'

'So –'

'So, I told De Jong, in spite of what he thought, I killed her. If it had not been for the argument –'

'But –' I insisted.

'Listen, listen,' he said softly. 'I know what you're going to say. They all said it in some way or other. They were very kind. They offered sympathy and compassion, which I accepted. But they felt like transient acquaintances. Like nice people you meet at a new port, who you will never see again. Strangers. They had no power to move me like she had.' His sad face was lit by the fire. Again it looked like gilded parchment. His hands were like talons.

I could see his fatigue. 'Shall I help you upstairs?'

'Yes,' he answered, to my surprise. Like a child, he allowed himself to be led away from the fire. 'It is gone now,' he said, so softly I could hardly hear him. 'And all I can do is try and remember.'

Through his eyes, I tried to see what he described. The winding staircase, the Long Room, the balcony with windows tilting outward.

On the landing, as we passed, he reached out a gnarled hand and touched the model of a ship, lightly, with one extended crooked finger.

A Cello

A man carrying a cello crossed the street. It was not in a case, its bare back was injured and its shoulders were covered in dust. Caked dust, raked with marks of fingers, as if someone had hastily brushed cobwebs and dirt away before it was taken into the street.

I stared at the instrument until it wobbled out of focus. The man disappeared and it seemed as if the cello moved on its own down Depiro Street. What was so striking about it?

I became suddenly faint, dizzy. When I finally lost sight of the cello, it was still there, etched in my sight like a blur in the eye that persists after looking at a very bright light. It was a kind of switch.

In a sense it was a Proustian twist, shooting me back to my childhood with such a backward rush, such momentum, I became disoriented. There, suddenly and inexplicably, was my father, in his shirtsleeves, smiling widely, as I do not remember having often seen him. There he stood, almost tangible, in a wide-yoked shirt with sleeves carefully rolled up to reveal powerful forearms covered in reddish hair. His boyish fringe fell like golden strings on a high forehead. He held a small broken violin and all around him were similarly damaged instruments. A burst snare drum, a clarinet without a mouthpiece, a guitar with cut cords curled and snarling, a tuba with a massive dent in its flare.

Instruments were grouped in his studio like survivors of some theatrical tragedy. But he was proud of them, of what they provided. Not music, of course, but a series of pictures he drew. Drawings appeared as suddenly in my mind as he had; a series of sketches, unframed, unmounted, stacked and piled, sheaved into portfolios. Excellent sketches of women holding different instruments. Whole instruments, bright and new-looking, gleaming with the potential of sound that promised to emit from their fingers, if only one could hear when they sat there, twanging strings, drawing a fine bow across the bridge of a violin, feathering a brush across the surface of a perfectly circular drum.

The women wore shining coiffures; their lips were lush and painted. Their faces were plump and smooth, their eyes half shut, delicious eyelashes lowered. And they were all naked. My mind swelled with images brought forth by the sight of the cello. I had only seen inside the studio a few times, and only in my very early childhood. It was now suddenly thrown open to me.

In my mind, I was hurled back, and tiptoed among grouped easels, stumbled over discarded smocks stained with paint, streaked with delicate colours of oil pastels. I felt the roll of a pencil under my heel, heard the crackle of old paper and smelled turpentine and linseed, dust, and stale sweet coffee forgotten in cups on a tray.

He spoke: 'You are not allowed in here.' The family was to keep out of the studio. He did make pictures of us, but he made them swiftly, brightly, in the open air.

He drew pictures of us playing together, of the baby on a blanket. He drew pictures of my brothers on my mother's lap as she sat on the shore. And of me alone, sitting on a rock with my skirt fanned out.

'You are not to come in here,' he said. And of course, now the reason seems obvious.

It becomes easy to see in hindsight what one was unable to comprehend as a child. It was because there was a naked woman on the couch, arms sensually draped around a dented tuba that would miraculously transform in the sketch to new: gleaming, superb in its roundness and wholeness. She, no matter how ill prepared for the sitting, would transform under his brush into a beautifully coiffed, sleek, dark creature groomed to perfection; a large chignon held in place by a rhinestone comb. Her teeth, no matter how uneven in life, would peep pearl-like, sketched between plump lips.

Where were those sketches? I stood straight on the balcony, allowing the gradual chill of evening to give me a small shiver. Closing the shutters and walking backwards into my room, I was reluctant to let my eyes fall upon my furniture, my stereo player, my neat shelf of books, lest they interrupted the memory. I was reluctant to let my father go. And the instruments. And the women ... the woman. That one dark beauty he sketched over and over again. Those sketches existed. They had to exist. They must have survived the intervening years, when my mind shed all remembrance of these things.

My father's trim moustache, his small smile and his strict tone telling me to shut the door behind me lived inside my head. All that survived. After such a death, after the punishment of forgetfulness, I had remembered and resurrected him. And her. And all it took was a glimpse of a cello crossing the street, dust raked across its shoulders exactly like on the one I saw in his studio so many years before.

I was a small girl, and dark, unlike my brothers. My eyelashes were thick and black. I know because my mother often exclaimed of their beauty to anyone who would listen. I would peep through the crack of the studio door that never closed properly because of an uneven architrave. I remember peeping and seeing nothing but a bright line of light. I remember hearing nothing but the tenor babble of my father's voice and the low sensual laughter of a female model whose presence was somehow commonplace. Whose presence was known to my mother, busy with four children, a cluttered household, a demanding kitchen and needlework of which she was so fond.

Suddenly now, I remember being chucked under the chin by that model. Tall, dark and vaguely amused by children, she was only momentarily distracted. My father hurried her into the studio, towards the old piano in the corner, and my mother said quickly, 'Come, let's all play in the kitchen.'

Now those are memories that have stuck fast. I need no prompting to recall the kitchen, my siblings, the sound of the kettle rattling its lid on full boil, the smell of rough-dried dishcloths, and the floury feel of a wooden spoon in my hand as I helped with the difficult mixing of some doughy stuff.

It is the other that suddenly bursts back to astonish, to daze. Did my mother really tolerate what went on in the studio? It was so close to where we all were, happily creating a domestic racket. Could the model really have been naked, clutching some broken instrument for the time it took my father to create a beautiful sketch in such detail? He renovated the instrument with his pencil. Created a gleam where there was none.

He re-coiffed the model, made up her lips, sheened her skin and lacquered her fingernails by the expedient of pencil and paper, pen and ink. He placed a genteel smile where there was none, under eyelids lowered in delightful modesty.

Where were those sketches? I thought once more of the man crossing the street with the cello – the cello with no case, no strings, and a fracture in its back. That back was beautiful once, like the back of an Ingres odalisque, like the back of my father's model.

The studio was the largest room of the apartment we had in Floriana. Light shot in directly from the sun whose face beamed at him as he sketched. It must have blinded the model as she sat; or my mother, as she bore the tray with cups of sweetened coffee. It was a cluttered dusty room, one I could just see if I racked my brain. I saw a clutch of dusty broken instruments, a wooden jointed doll that never really took the place of a model, a heap of rags in a corner, a drum of turpentine without a cap. I could just see an oil lamp with a sooty glass, a thick velvet curtain to one side of the window, its hem draped over a rattan stool. A pile of sketches. A cello. A drum. A head of black hair. A thigh, a breast.

Was it a genuine memory? Was I conjuring images? Did I remember a cat? A small vision of a grey cat slunk in the corner of my mind but I could not be sure. All I saw was the rosy flank of a model undressing, her hips curved and her arms raised to free her head of her blouse. All I saw were arms angled as she gathered black hair into the semblance of a chignon, which in my father's picture would be faultless, like the sheen on her lips.

All I saw was my father's eyes as he nodded her towards the seat and the waiting tuba, and his hands as he guided her arms around the instrument and asked her to sit like that. And like that. And I saw – or sensed – my mother's eyes lower, her head turn, and her mouth open to summon us into the warm kitchen where we would be together and play and cook and sing our childhood songs.

'You are not allowed in here,' he said.

So I stayed out. But I must have seen those pictures. I remembered seeing those pictures. There were dozens. I could almost hear the hiss and scrape of pencil on paper as he created them, although I could never have stood close enough for that. The apartment was a noisy place. My mother sang, we children clattered and rattled and shouted our every emotion with unbridled gusto.

I remembered the hot streaming of my own tears and shouts bellowed from my chest and throat when I closed my fingers in the hot oven door one day, surreptitiously attempting to taste some delicacy. I recalled the shrill protests I emitted when my brothers wrested a wooden bird from my hands and 'flew' it onto the roof of the house next door. And the bawling of the new baby.

'You are not allowed in here.'

Was that the only time I saw him in shirtsleeves? I remembered a thick tweed jacket and its rough smoky fragrance as he lifted me up the stairs, drowsy and inert after an exhausting day in the country. There was a black suit he wore to court, a light brown jacket he wore on racing days. There was the smell of horses, the smell of salt in his hair when he went to cafés on the sea front, the smell of turpentine and linseed that lingered around the door of the studio. There was a jacket he painted in on cold winter days, whose cuffs were threadbare and greasy.

We were not allowed in there, but I must have seen those pictures. I wondered whether my brothers had similar images in their store of memories. Whether they too suppressed the recollection of a naked woman clutching a dusty violin, an unstrung guitar, or the dented tuba. Whether they knew what happened to the sketches.

The day my father died, I admitted to relief. Sighs exploded from my chest as I thought of him released at last from the pain and the silence. He had not sketched for years, of course. The nuns who cared for him would sometimes place a pencil in the fingers on his left side, the side that was still whole, and he would produce childlike scribbles and a brilliant smile. The end was long and cruel, leaving me breathless and exhausted.

If I called Joseph, would he tell me where the sketches were? Or Bart, or Philip? Perhaps they had clear memories of the model, of my mother's inscrutable self-effacing tact.

'We all have different ways of remembering,' Bart said dismissively, the time we all met after the reading of my father's will, when coming together again after such a long time was awkward and I tried conversationally to cheer him up with recollections of our boisterous childhood.

'It's almost as if you weren't there, Severine,' added Philip, giving me an absurd scolding then for how I had been as a child. 'It was awful sometimes. The way you talk makes it all sound like the happy stories of some other family.'

Joseph remained silent, but one arched eyebrow seemed to confirm what the other two said: it was awful sometimes. Was I the only one with fond warm memories of the Floriana flat, of our kitchen, of light streaking through the gap of the ill-fitting studio door over our small heads as we played?

I tried to reach my brothers, still in my daze of new memory. Joseph was not home, but Philip picked up his telephone almost at once.

'What sketches?' he asked at first.

I realised he was annoyed, pretending not to know what I was talking about.

'Come on, Philip,' I urged. 'You know exactly what sketches. What happened to all Dad's work?'

'You really don't remember, do you?'

'No, I don't!' I was annoyed now at his silly evasion.

'You were always unobservant, happy and all wrapped up in yourself,' he said, without holding back now. 'You always found something to be happy about. All that was going on, with you in the middle of it, and you don't even remember when Mama...' he stopped.

There was silence on the line. If I said nothing he would continue, I hoped.

'Look – there are no sketches, Severine.'

'No sketches?' It was impossible. My mind held precise images of them. Explicit detail. They had to exist. I had seen them.

'Think back,' he said with exasperation in his voice. 'You were about ... nine? It was the middle of summer. That woman Annette...'

'Annette?'

'The model. She had just left. Mama was in tears again. Accusing. Pleading with Dad again. It was unbearable. Noisy, like everything else this family did. It was a noisy argument, more like a fight.'

'A fight!' I exclaimed.

'They were always fighting, Severine. This is something else you cannot seem to remember. Mama's voice was unbearable. Dad was in a rage, his eyes bulging like they did when he was drinking.' He paused again.

I took a deep breath but resolved not to speak. My father, drinking? To cling to my own memories of him now would be sentimental. I shut my eyes and held my breath. If I wanted the truth, I would have to listen to Philip.

He went on. 'Dad started shouting. Yes, yes yes! He kept saying yes at the top of his voice for a long time. All the time it took him to drag all his pictures out of the studio and down into the street. Everything – sketches, canvases, easel – the lot. He dragged it all out onto the pavement outside and set fire to it – then and there, right in the middle of Granaries Street.'

He heard me inhale sharply, but did not stop. 'The only reason he was not arrested was because he was so well known, and they all knew how patiently our mother had put up... Look – it would have been yet another embarrassment, Severine.'

I put the telephone down gently. The flat behind me was in complete darkness. I went out onto the balcony again and stood in the diffused glow from a nearby street light, half expecting the man with the cello to return that way, wending his way past me in reverse, attempting to erase it all with his long black shadow. Philip was right, I remembered nothing, and striving for recall now would be stupid. I did not want a sordid memory of sad selfishness and indulgence, jealousy and tears. I wanted desperately to retain the memories I had of warmth and rowdy family happiness, of bohemian untidiness relieved by artistic splendour, but I sensed it would be impossible. If I thought about it, if I concentrated, it would all come back. And I did not want it to.

Il Funerale di un Vescovo

Paolo was at the station in Grosseto. 'Kate! Welcome.'

I expected humour but found awkwardness. I sensed anxiety and fretfulness beneath his wide smile. His greeting was too loud, his laugh nervous. He spoke quickly about Lucia, about their casale where Armand was painting.

'Do you need a coffee?' he asked solicitously.

My skirt was creased after hours in a train, my hair was hidden under my felt hat, my throat was parched, but I wanted to be taken to the casale immediately.

'Armand practically lives with us now, you know.' Paolo settled into the driver's seat. 'At first, he lodged in the village, now he has a room with us. Lucia and I treat him as part of the furniture. Is that what you say, part of the furniture?'

I smiled, one eye on the scenery and the other on Paolo's flighty driving. Even in this part of the Maremma, it was busy. I expected relief from crowds, noise and the pollution of cities I visited in the last four months. In a way, it was there: in the grey-green of hills, the soft buzz of bees. And in faces of children, who seemed less predatory here.

Paolo interrupted with information in a mixture of English, Italian and French, saying breathlessly how Armand bent their wishes, evolved their ideas for the painting until it became a frieze; then a full mural, until it became a fresco covering all four walls in the dining hall.

'Wasn't it once a friary?' I asked about the house.

'Who knows about these old places?' He shrugged and pulled an eloquent face. 'Hearsay, myth – not reliable except for what it is.'

'But Lucia wrote...' I started, and thought of her long letters filled with description, history, and a lot of elaboration in reply to my own boring notes.

'Lucia believes what she likes to believe,' he laughed. His breathing became laboured, as if we ascended on foot. At the house, I was impressed by thick limestone walls, a rampart-like rooftop, and glimpses of a more ancient ruin through trees.

Lucia waved from the doorway. 'Benvenuta!' Her voice carried easily in the limpid air of late afternoon. She too seemed breathless, but led me eagerly to what she called the refettorio. 'Armand is dying to meet you.' She fumbled for a cigarette.

'You said I was coming?'

She cocked an eyebrow through smoke. 'Do you think he'd allow a complete stranger see the funeral?'

Funeral? I had no time to ask. We entered an archway lit by a fluorescent tube lying on the floor. Wires snaked around us, leading to lights scattered over the floor of a vast chamber.

'Armand!' Her voice was loud and metallic in the space. Paolo was already there. He introduced us expansively.

I shook the artist's hand, looking around. 'I never thought it was so large.'

'Why do you think it's taking all these years?' Lucia's voice grated.

Perhaps Armand was costing too much. He looked dwarfed, and the light bent his frame. He was bent. I looked at his back before I could stop myself. I wanted him to be glad I arrived but there was no sign of that kind of feeling. 'Show me,' I said. Lights on the floor lit trestles and ladders that hid the mural. Armand pulled a couple back with some effort, and Paolo rushed to help.

I was dumbfounded for a minute. The painted scene before me seemed jumbled, its colours ran together, shadows of ladders and trestles crisscrossed figures and crowds.

Eventually, a kind of sequence, of clarity, emerged as I tried to understand. It was huge: from knee-height to lofty ceiling, along four irregular walls.

'I won't ask what you think,' said Armand, after I stood in silence for some time.

'But she'll tell you!' exclaimed Paolo. He laughed and patted my shoulder, ending nervously with another laugh. Paolo obviously learned about my directness from Lucia, with whom I spent many years at convent-school. Now eager to make me welcome, he was like a puppy.

Armand climbed a trestle.

'He will describe it now,' said Lucia, through the exhaled smoke of another cigarette.

'Hey! Are we smoking in here now?' Armand's voice reverberated through the hall.

Lucia disappeared through the archway.

'The funeral of a bishop!' Armand made his announcement, arms flung wide.

'*Il funerale di un vescovo*, more properly,' said Paolo.

Armand ignored him. 'Look, Kate – see why it has taken almost five years! I started there. Yes, behind you. At first, I stencilled figures onto plaster, I didn't know what it was to be, but I had to have crowds. Crowds! I made cartoons of characters from two villages. Yes, they sat for me. I made profiles, frontals. See? Children, village elders, animals.'

71

The scene behind me lived. Colours, although confused by strange light, vibrated. A man with a fur collar held aloft a pear-shaped cheese, offering it for sale, mouth wide, showing irregular teeth. Smiling children gathered around kittens on the ground. Feet milled together; skirts and coat hems twirled and met; shoulders bumped and grinded; heads nodded, and turned to look at a procession.

'When I started the procession,' the artist continued, 'it was already winter, the second year!' Brush in hand, he related exuberantly how he looked for faces in villages, and disappeared for days in Lucia's car.

'He returned with sketches,' said Paolo. 'We'd hold them against the wall and Armand would say Here! And here! And here! They took weeks to be translated – transformed into what you see.'

I saw priests in albs and cassocks, holding banners overhead. There were bald pates, tonsures, the ruddy skin of well-fed Italian monks. Expectant crowds lined the painted street, agape at the pageantry. There were blonde heads, dark faces, almond eyes, a close crowd of shapes and skins of different origins. One woman held a holy picture, hand frozen in the sign of the cross, black veil hiding half a pious face. Next to her stood the eccentric figure of a clown, dressed for a carnival, whose jingle bells almost tinkled, shining on the hem of red and yellow satin, which had seen better days. He waved a spiralled baton, but his painted smile did not quite hide black stubble and a toothless scowl.

'This is magnificent.' I was astonished. What I expected from Lucia's written description was a bucolic scene of Maremma peasants enjoying the country. I thought I would see grapevines, maidens and baskets of produce: not this strange mixture of faces and bodies jostling each other. 'Why a funeral?' My curiosity could not be contained. 'And where is the...'

'The coffin!' Armand exclaimed and jumped to the ground. I feared for his back. He saw my look. 'Don't worry, I've heard all the Michelangelo jokes. Yes, I've twisted and turned on scaffolding for four years, but it's my eyes, not my back, that hurt.' He took my arm and led toward the archway.

'There is no coffin,' Paolo mumbled. They both looked at the blank part of the wall.

I looked at Armand.

'No coffin yet,' he said, with an apologetic grin. 'I – uh, it's difficult. I cannot bring myself to ...'

We sat around the dinner table in a blur of conversation, at the edges of which I felt a strange tautness. They were too nice to each other, all for my benefit.

Fruit, cheese and what Lucia termed 'something English for a change', in a casserole, were served on colourful plates. They asked about my trip, the stay in Rome, but I had patience for nothing but the mural.

'It had to be a funeral?' I asked, not hiding my fascination.

'Yes, Kate,' said Armand, waving a piece of cheese held expressively in two fingers. 'But it is not about death. Funerals are about life, about the surge of a wave inward, quick and sudden, to fill a void created by the previous wave...' He moved impatiently, in frustration, lost for words.

I thought then I knew what he meant. 'It also is about the futility of belief and necessity of ritual,' said Lucia suddenly. She had not spoken for a while, quiet at the head of the table. She covered the earthenware casserole and looked across at Paolo.

Again, I felt a strange tension, now more apology than hostility.

'Lucia, Lucia,' laughed Armand. He munched cheese, and raised eyes to ceiling. 'Aren't women wonderful?' He spoke to Paolo, who was too engrossed in Lucia to respond. Then he continued, 'I am a painter, not a philosopher!'

'It's true, Armand,' she answered. 'But you must admit your vision and slant on life have a message. Um – a theme...' Lucia looked to Paolo for help.

'Unity, perhaps? Understanding?' Paolo suggested.

All of a sudden, there was a flood of forgiveness tangible as the cheese and Faenza plates. Whatever obstacle had stood between them now evaporated away. I was surprised at my own intuitive relief, but what they exuded was plain, tangible.

Armand continued to chatter about the mural, talking about the mathematical difficulty of two-thirds scale, how paint had to be remixed in stages, a lot of technicality.

Lucia and Paolo were lost in their private silence.

'I want you to understand something.' The artist did not sense a thing. He gulped the last of the red wine and stood. He led me with a gesture of his head to the great hall. We left them behind, and I listened for the murmur of their voices as we drew away.

'Here.' Armand's voice was once more metallic, and rattled in the vastness. 'Here I'll paint the catafalque, borne by twelve deacons – capes of purple, all that. Behind them, altar boys.' He held a hand at the height of phantom heads. 'They will bear sheaves of grain and arum lilies. And here …' His hand flew to point in the sky, 'a flight of grey pigeons released from cane cages … down here, where three little urchins kneel.'

I saw it all, although the spaces on the walls were merely prepared with cream impasto marked with dots of charcoal. 'And of course, most important of all – the face of the dead bishop.' Armand's voice hushed suddenly to impress significance.

'Of course.'

'I'll paint it rosy, smiling, calm and relieved, like in a quick, peaceful siesta on a hot afternoon! A face merely asleep, lined with signs of work and laughter.'

I looked at this bent man, his vivid eyes, black hair, and expressive gestures. What he described was a strong face, a dynamic one.

Lucia came back and led me away to the garden to show me her work. She straightened a cigarette on the back of a hand, lit it, squinted round at me and showed me gardenias, crumbling walls festooned with morning glory, great bushes of geraniums she called *Sardinella*.

There was nothing exotic about the grounds. All the plants were commonplace, but grew lush and vigorous, crowding the paths and filling stone urns to overflowing. The star shaped glossy leaves of a lilac geranium brushed her head as she led under a walkway toward the grotto. I knew it was there from her letters.

'Armand...' she started.

I wanted to say, 'You've had an affair with him, haven't you?' The words caught in my throat when I saw her eyes, and stayed there. Instead, I said, 'What about Armand?' like a stranger.

'He's been diagnosed,' she said. 'You know... positive.'

I gasped. We entered the grotto and the sharp smell of mould made me exhale quickly. Lucia turned suddenly, stopping in her tracks to face me.

I did not know what to say.

'See the moisture?' She broke the discomfort that enfolded us with something that had nothing to do with the artist or his work. 'The water runs down the sides of the cave, leaving colour behind.'

'A natural kind of mural,' I said lamely.

'Do you like it here? It's cool – stay, relax.' She left me there, and I made my way back to the house, after about ten minutes, seeing it this time from another angle, in the twilight, angered by the way she sprang Armand's news on me, saddened by the fate of this complete stranger whose bent form, brilliant eyes and mysterious painting had already struck me indelibly.

I wound my way back to the refettorio, losing my way twice. It was dark when I entered, so the fluorescent lights on the floor blinded me for a second. I tripped over snaking wires, righted myself and looked up.

Armand was on the scaffolding, with his back to me. He must have heard my noise, but continued to trace a shape onto the wall. 'That you, Lucia?'

Again, I was made to feel uncomfortable. 'No,' I said, too loudly, too quickly, so he wouldn't say to me anything intended for her ears only. 'No, it's me, Kate.'

He turned, smiling a welcome. Could he see the difference in me now? That I knew about his condition?

He jumped down, and winced on landing unsteadily, as I winced, when I looked at his back.

He pointed, without a word, so we looked together on the crowd, and I started to notice the fine detail in the silence we maintained. There was litter among the forest of feet, stray cats and a lost shoe. The hands were expressive, managing to convey the class, occupation and gender of the characters to which they belonged. I saw calluses, tapering nails, scratches, rings, wrinkles and the stains of ink and beetroot.

Armand was full of the bishop's appearance. He led me to the blank space where the cleric would lie. Eagerly, he reached for a battered roll of paper. It looked like greaseproof paper, and bore creases and dents. He had worked on whatever it was for a long time. He unrolled it, and placed it on the floor, holding the dog-eared corners down with lights, cable, a case of brushes, and a tin of paint.

I looked, craning from my standing position.

'See?' He spoke slowly, although I could feel his tension. He knew I knew. 'See? His face will be full of a well-fed kind of complacency. Peace,' he said.

'Lined with signs of work and laughter, you said before.' I said the words quietly.

He was pleased I remembered. He seemed eager to show me something. Something he could not put into words.

The sketch on the roll of paper was a masterpiece itself, and eloquent. He had no need now to point out the irony of what he intended. It was clear and I saw it plainly. I looked at a tracery of lines around the dead bishop's mouth, and understood immediately. Armand was going to paint his own face.

A Great Intimacy

Upstairs, Judah was packing books. The sky had hardly lightened yet. Curtains were tightly drawn and for all the world, it was night time in the brown house.

'He wants to leave while it is all still muted. Before the colour comes out to hold him here,' Enid said quietly to herself.

Perhaps she knew she had no way of detaining him any longer. Perhaps she knew France was only one of the detours he was making on a journey he had described as a loop, a circle to whose beginning he must return. She felt as grey and featureless as the fields outside. If Judah could see them, if he would only pull the curtains back, he would see the dawn bring some vestige of colour to the fields, and to the grey skin on Enid's cheeks.

Halfway up the stairs, caught between treads, she did not know whether to return downstairs or to continue upward; to where rustling noises and the smell of disturbed mothballs advertised an imminent departure. Panic held her to the spot. The panic of indecision and that of desolation she sensed in the weeks to come.

Judah had painted the brown house. And the Dieppe fields. He filled spreads of Masonite with flat expanses of dull grey; 'the most difficult colour', he would say, as he interspersed fields of fine dots with two or three splashes of green.

He painted her, too; an oblong in the middle distance whose human form could only be made out if one squinted and looked through gathered eyelashes and the miraging of eyelids.

'Is it really me?' She had asked in an empty kind of tone, but naked hope still filled the small room he turned into a studio. It seeped out onto the landing where she was supposed to wait until he said she could enter. She had brought tray upon tray of jugged water and dry biscuits.

'Don't you want anything else?' she asked.

'Not while I'm working. And yes, it is you.' He mumbled, and his tone sounded irritated. She knew it was his natural air. He always spoke like that.

'You walked out there a couple of days ago in that dull white dress and from the window you seemed to pull the far end of the field with you.'

Now, Judah talked with his face in the packing case. His books were all inside it; and his brushes, paints, flat cases of knives and tubes. 'I do not want to leave a mess for you.'

The room was taking on the shape and smell of before he had arrived.

Enid's tentative voice filled the space she was reluctant to leave empty. 'Will you take the scenery with you?'

Judah looked up as if startled, his eyebrows almost met over his nose, and a slight tremble reached the crease between his lip and his left cheek.

Anger, thought Enid. She angered him without wanting to, but it was extremely difficult to have any sort of conversation with the strange Australian without risking some kind of conflict.

'Of course not,' he replied. 'Do you think Fred Williams took anything of France back with him when he was here?' His voice was neither that of lecturer nor of friend nor tenant. It rose, cracking audibly like a twig underfoot as he continued. 'There is the pleasure of rediscovering the familiar, after a long and often lonely period abroad...'

Lonely: Enid winced involuntarily.

'There's the shock of recognition,' he said, unmoved. 'Do you think Williams, on first seeing Fremantle after his absence, did not thrill to see the land – his landscape? I told you once.' He shuddered with what Enid took to be extreme impatience with her forgetfulness. 'I told you it was one of the most important reasons I came to Europe to start with.'

'So that you could return,' she said blankly.

'Return and see. Return and see, Enid.'

Downstairs, Enid shrugged away the feeling of stupidity, and took on instead the sense of renewed excitement she had every time he remembered to use her name.

Adolescent, she thought. Stupid, stupid and young: when would she ever learn?

In the kitchen, light filtered through the blind and a streak of yellow lit up blue cups she had set out earlier. In the quiet, Enid could hear the distant voice of waves against chalk cliffs. She considered herself lucky to be able to afford this abandoned farmhouse in Dieppe, with the money her English parents were thoughtful enough to have saved and left her. She considered the novelty of taking boarders, English speaking boarders, quaint and almost Victorian.

Financially, it had not been an altogether successful venture. Personally, she found she soaked all her visitors with her loneliness, swamping them with attention and a kind of sticky care she saw well-meaning volunteers drench on animals at the Manchester pound where she had worked for a while.

Full of disgust with herself at displaying so much loneliness, Enid would withdraw and take to the fields, or to the cliffs, for a glimpse of the clutch of buildings gathered near the edge, which would make everything worse, everything lonelier.

Judah painted those houses, roughly, savagely, imitating what Williams had made of the scene, he said, when he was there in 1956.

Nineteen fifty-six, the year after she was born. Enid poured hot water into the coffee pot and waited for the coffee grounds to become saturated. She pushed the plunger down mechanically after the prescribed wait, during which she tapped a single finger on her kitchen table. So Judah wanted what he said Williams had experienced on his return to Australia all those years ago. She had never heard of Fred Williams until this Australian stood on her doorstep several months ago, saying he had seen her card on the board at the delicatessen in town. 'It was a surprise seeing a notice in English,' he had said with a smile that seemed infrequently tried, with that mouth.

Enid smoothed her short hair needlessly, frowned about her old t-shirt and shorts and looked as closely as she dared at his own crumpled clothes, the short beard and dull grey eyes, which the smile had failed to reach.

She never heard of Fred Williams, or of Fremantle. Judah stared in disbelief at her ignorance as he described Western Australia, his home state, to her. He showed her pictures and   photographs of the desert, of seascapes and rivers seen from such enormous distances they seemed meagre rather than grand. He showed her posters, prints and book illustrations of Williams's paintings; strange map-like pictures whose flatness grew into mental similarities and imaginings which were a new experience for her. They were more mental than visual. She said so and he stared at her vacantly.

'Williams wanted to make of landscape painting something solid and enduring as the art of museums,' Judah had said.

Understanding all of his words but little of the intense meaning that was their obvious source, Enid felt frustration and stupidity flood her.

Judah painted for days at a time in one of the rooms he rented from her upstairs. He would take a sketchpad and wander out sometimes, heedless of the weather. She stood in the kitchen and watched him prepare to leave in the rain one morning. Enid had said, 'It was beautiful yesterday,' to which Judah had growled in response, as if to say she must have no notion of what was beautiful.

Was there nothing she could say to him that did not evoke friction? Rather than friction, it was awkwardness, a taut feeling of intense discomfort. They never really fought.

'You agree with everything I say!' He shouted in dismay one twilit evening as they ate dinner in the courtyard. She had draped vine leaves over a red and white checked tablecloth and the broken half of a baguette had fallen to the tiled floor as he rose angrily from the table. 'Australian women at least give you some sort of a decent debate.'

'Debate?' she repeated stupidly. She knew nothing of Australian women, or of making sport of argument. Her parents had shown her how to make conversation smooth and pleasant, how to complement a visitor's words with polite inquiry. Never be inquisitive or probing, Enid's mother had taught. Now she was being requested to quarrel, to argue and negate. They were talking about landscape again; the Australian landscape, which Judah had been trying to 'borrow'.

'Borrow, not capture.' He stressed his words and cupped his hands as if to illustrate how he wanted to do it.

Enid nodded.

'Williams avoided what he termed view painting. He did not make picture postcards. He made solid pictorial effects, emphasising individual form rather than diffusing it into the contemporary concept of what was abstract.' The artist continued his monologue, stressing individual words as if to imprint them on not only Enid's mind but also his own, as if teaching himself something in the process. It was what he told her he learnt when he lectured at the art college he had hated so.

'I would talk and talk,' he said, confiding in her without giving her a sense of intimacy. 'I found myself shouting a lecture so that I was hoarse when I got home. I was aggressive, wanting all to embrace my opinions without even forming or considering their own. I raved, Enid. I raved and strode around, finding at the end I learnt much more from my own words than any of them did.'

'I'm sure some found your instruction useful.' It was the only thing she found to say.

He looked at her blankly. 'Instruction? Useful? What do you mean you're *sure*?'

Alone in her room much later, Enid thought of his near obsession as she stared at a poster she just tacked on her wall. You Yangs 1965, it was titled. Judah had given her the poster and she unrolled it slowly. She flattened it on the kitchen table, seeing only a series of dots, streaks and small splashes at first. She did not know what You Yangs meant.

When she asked, Judah rattled off a series of names. Olinda, Upwey, Echuca, Sherbrooke, You Yangs, Werribee, Guthega. 'Places in Victoria.' His lecturer's voice filled the kitchen. 'The You Yangs was where Williams found his breakthrough style – which would make him instantly recognisable. He embraced the challenge of finding form in a seemingly featureless landscape. He found he could transform familiar landscape motifs into a new pictorial experience.'

Enid looked at the poster on her wall. Judah said Williams had painted it in a studio. It was a re-experienced landscape, he said. That was why she asked if he would take her part of the world back with him to Australia. She wondered about the place that had inspired the dabs and dashes, but knew she would never ask.

'I am going to fly back into Western Australia,' Judah had said quietly the day before the packing began.

That was when Enid knew he was leaving. It was abrupt, a hint of a departure she had not even dared to hope against.

'I'm going to get a topographic view of the land around Perth, he said, with longing – or apprehension – in his voice. 'The land around Broome. From a great height, I will see what has been hidden from me for a long time. I am going to feel that *aha!* of recognition and I am going to incubate it.'

'Then you will paint it?'

'It will be my Sherbrooke, you understand.' He mumbled, for the first time not contradicting Enid when she offered words. She realised suddenly he hardly saw her, hardly looked at her. Alone in the kitchen, she stood and poured more coffee into her own cup. His was still empty, awaiting his descent from the room where rustling of paper seemed furtive and the cloud of disturbed dust attacked the nostrils.

For an instant, Enid thought of letters, of writing. She remembered pictures she had been shown in which Williams's daubs had resembled handwriting. Indecipherable letters on a dull dun background filled her head as she sat back on the old country chair and closed her eyes. She saw a beige picture Judah showed her in a book: Australian Landscape I 1960-70.

It had startled her with its emptiness, its careful spread of uniform colour speckled here and there with coloured dots and blotches. The eloquence of the scene had disturbed her. The streaks were neither trees nor people, but they meant life. Their precise placement on the landscape became suddenly meaningful to her in a way she could not say in words.

'It is a symbolic code.' Judah explained what he saw, but she saw the life, the movement and the exact choreography the artist had used.

When he left, there was no solemn leave-taking. She stayed up in her small room and waited for the noisy bumping he made, taking boxes and cases down to the waiting taxi. She waited for the noise to stop. She sat on her wooden bed and waited. He would come up and knock, she thought; he would offer her his hand as he had done when he arrived all those months ago. He would smile a smile at once cheerful and apologetic, as he had once when he spilled a jar of honey on her linen tablecloth. 'Did you embroider this yourself?' He was unusually polite and formal.

'No, no,' she said dismissively. 'I bought this at an antique shop in town. They are vine leaves, see.'

Judah brought the honey-stained cloth almost to his lips and looked closely at the embroidery, squinting his eyes. 'Either a great distance or a great intimacy,' he said. 'Both change how the eyes see things.' He had said intimacy: not closeness, not proximity. The word stayed with her for a long time, making her examine their time together. There had been intimacy of sorts, when they ate together, in the kitchen on rainy days with the stove door open for warmth. He had peeled figs and grapes for her with his artist's fingers. He had once even folded all her dry washing from the line, placing her small rolled-up underwear on top of the pile.

He had repeated place names in Western Australia until they became familiar to her. Arthur River, Jerramungup, Corrigin, Willyabrup, Port Hedland. She would repeat them to herself and picture them as dots, daubs and splashes on backgrounds of map-like whorls. He laughed at her hesitancy with the unusual words, the humour never quite reaching his eyes. His fingers played with crumbs or the blue handle of a teaspoon. His dull grey eyes followed her but he never joined her when she crossed the fields.

'I'm off then!' He shouted from the bottom of the stairs. The distant voice startled Enid. She was expecting a soft scrape from the doorknob.

'Look me up when you come to Broome or Perth!' he ended. Or Esperance or Port Hedland or Margaret River,

91

she thought dully. Then she rose quickly to her feet. Panic swamped her and confusion made her trip over her own feet. By the time she reached the bottom stair, from where he had called, the taxi was crunching rapidly on the gravel at the end of her path. Enid ran to the door and waved at the retreating car, feeling silly and regretful. He must have thought she did not want to say goodbye.

She found a painting on the kitchen table, a small square of Masonite that held a vertical clutch of lines ticked here and there with gold and green. It was a forest, she thought, a woods like the one at the bottom of the fields. She looked at the lines for a long time, watching the dots become birds and then leaves and then motes of sunlight. In the corner of the picture, she noticed a small cream oblong, a human shape that seemed to walk along the border and through the trees.

Reference: Patrick McCaughey *Fred Williams* Bay Books 1980

Twenty Minutes, Two Years

As he becomes intoxicated, Geffron lifts his eyes over the horizon he has created out of the windowsill. It is pockmarked and stripped of any paint. His eyes seem to search, but really, he is too far gone to see with any clarity.

If I lean to look from his perspective, I see only the corner of the street where a bollard stands on the cantonade. I see the windows, closed and barred, of the bakery and the wine-seller's threshold. The street is deserted, but perhaps he sees something in his delirium.

Geffron is dog-tired, but he is too heavy and uncooperative for me to lead up the stone stairs from this basement. We will both tumble if I undertake to lend him my shoulder. I am afraid I have had the lion's share of the first bottle, and although I hardly sip from my only glass from the second, he throws his head back with his.

Geffron is wearing his father's jacket, and the trousers he borrowed from me and retained ownership of in his drunken forgetfulness. He is thinking of her – 'She.' He does not remember that she does not turn that corner any more, and even if she did, he could not possibly see her.

The room is quiet, and my dog, that was scratching itself so vigorously only half an hour ago, lies still now and twitches with the infrequent passage of a rat through its dreams.

My dog, Geffron and I: it has been two years now that we form this inadequate and unlikely trio. They hate each other, and I – I love them both with the stubbornness and frustration of being unable to do anything about what has gone before. And with the impotence to change what else lies ahead.

He has stopped mumbling in his stupor, and looks at the dog. He nods in the animal's direction and starts to say something, but he either smells his own breath and stops, or is unable to remember the words that go with his thought. Again, his head lobs backward, and then abruptly forward, like one nodding off to sleep, but I know he will not pass into sleep; neither peaceful slumber nor thrashing nightmares will claim him before he slumps unconscious.

His uneven beard rests on his dirty shirtfront. One of his eyes is closed. I am too tired myself and much too cautious to make sudden noise to place another of the logs on the fire. We shall sit here in the gathering darkness and cold of a spent and ashy fire, whose unstirred embers and damp wood have stunk and spluttered all night. I do not see signs of dawn, because the window faces the wrong direction for that, and it is only now I notice that one of the street lamps on that corner has not come on at all tonight.

The whole quarter is sinking into a seediness and dilapidation that is comforting. It matches, somehow, the state of Geffron and of my dog, and yes, perhaps of the sadness I have sunk into myself. I cannot help hoping she would not turn that corner; even if the very idea is ridiculous. To hope for the impossible *not* to happen is a contradiction, whose terms I have denied for years. When she left for the big cities – who know which ones? – the whole town knew it was because of the rivalry Geffron and I had presented her with.

We did not even give her the necessary hope of a choice. It was a rivalry she could do nothing about, and her whole life seemed ruled by it: but only for the few months in which it grew into a ridiculous feud, dividing the drinking crowds into factions of absurdity.

For a while, she revelled in its flattery, but realisation of the actual meaning of the damaged personalities behind the rivalry left her little to be proud of.

Geffron is shifting uncomfortably in his chair and my dog growls in its shallow sleep. They both shift in their semi-consciousness and, as usual, I am the one who is the most alert, the one who digests what we have created for ourselves. The bottle has been pushed to the far end of the table, by either my hand or his. It is too late to distinguish us now.

No one has turned on the lights in this corner of the bar, and who would wish to approach such unkempt and incoherent characters? Again, I wonder whether I should risk injury by carrying him up the stairs. I have grazed many a knee on those stone steps, and rested many a shaky elbow on the wooden balustrade whose newel seems eroded. Indeed, a river has washed around it year after year, one of loneliness and disillusion, of unlikely rapports between men of different pasts and fates.

I wonder whether I should risk the noise of kicking the fire. Geffron charges when provoked with noise, or with the threat of unrest about him.

How we threw ourselves together was, in hindsight, inevitable. We were the only two willing to pitch our hopelessness against each other's.

We were the only two whose rage and noise were somehow equal. First we were sworn rivals, vying for the same woman, pushing each other into arguments and drinking bouts whose results are forgotten by all save her, who is now gone. How she could have borne the company of either of us after those pub nights is a mystery. Then we realised her absence had confirmed the stupidity of futile contending, and we would sit in maudlin talk, omitting her name as if the whole occurrence were about some other hypothetical woman. Our garbled, inebriated talk was decipherable only to each other, so we would help each other up the stone steps until it was never clear which one of us was the worse for drink.

The dog is up and scratches at a door that has not, to my knowledge, been opened for years. I think there is a counter pushed up against it in the other room, where we have eaten and brawled together. Precariously, I lean over and push open the one that leads to the lobby, and the bright light blinds me for an instant, the dog slinks past me. There are still a few jackets and coats on the hooks out there, and I can hear voices.

Geffron stirs. He hears the dog's claws click on the floorboards, and light from the door slants past his elbow. He is trying to rise from the chair. These days it takes him much less time to get drunk, and much longer to recover. His sight is permanently impaired. With long standing habit, he reaches for my arm and pulls.

He has not even the shadow of a doubt that I would be there. I let him pull: he is too weak to move me. He will tire and sag back against the bow back of his chair.

I look into the street again to adjust my vision to darkness and the safety of grey. My eyes are at pavement level. There is a man out there now. I recognise his walk and the way his coat flaps about his knees. My dog is out there too, and sniffs him as he walks towards a corner. He reels slightly, but is not too self-occupied to notice one of the lamps is out, and looks up. He remains immobile with his chin pointing upwards and a shaky finger half indicating the direction of the lamp in the slow motions of the very drunk. I can almost pin point the moment he will move again.

I am not so sober I can damn Fillippi out there, but somehow I feel I must shake either Geffron or myself into action of some sort. We stagger together. All lights seem to have gone out at once and there is a momentary lapse between artificial glow and that from the yellow dawn behind us, over the top of the Bourse building and the old cinema.

I can hear commotion and cries from the direction of the markets. Geffron mumbles but he cannot walk and talk at the same time. His other hand reaches out for some imaginary arm. Perhaps her arm, for she often took him home: took me home, too. My suits were smarter then, my shirts ironed. I was clean-shaven, and because of my three years advantage over him, thought I had a better chance.

He says something about foghorns when we stop at that corner, and he leans dreadfully over the bollard. The wall is blackened all the way round by night hands finding their way. She used to turn the corner suddenly, curving her ankles smartly, like a model.

Geffron's chin is tucked into my shoulder. The baker is opening his shop, his apprentice already covered in flour. My head is clearing and sounds from the market now mix with those from the canals: the static shout of the hawker mingles with the transient promise of the bargee.

I can imagine young sailors running the dawn flags up, quickly tying thin new ropes and secreting their first cigarette of the day. I am ill with the image and the sharp smell of morning.

Geffron reels and leans on my reliable arm, his grip spasmodic. His jacket reeks of his father's salumerie: smoked eel and dried sausage. His fingers are those of a wharf worker, but he has not worked for years. He has not worked since she left; since she told all at the pub of her intention to explore the cities.

Geffron remembers her red coat, but he does not mention it. Only, when a woman in a similar coat comes into the bar, he quickly orders another round or asks Oscar for the bottle. Our liaison has eliminated other relationships. I no longer seek the company of bar women, and he dismisses even the possibility of conversation with visitors to the basement salon.

He has started to look paunchy, and much older than he should. Few believe he has a father: alive, successful and as sober as a stockbroker. Few believe he once wore sailor's fatigues, fresh and neat as his folded hammock. But that was where his drinking started, and relegation to dock work seemed almost appropriate. I see him now as he was when I met him; he sees me not at all.

Waking is when we avoid each other, and it becomes increasingly difficult. We share the very room I used to take her to. Perhaps she played us against each other as young women often do. If it worked, it must be in contradiction of her intentions. We are inseparable now, out of guilt as well as out of necessity.

He suddenly takes charge in a sharp moment of lucidity that vanishes as quickly as it comes, and he lets go of my elbow when I am fumbling for the key which was once mine but which now lives in his fetid pocket.

Absentmindedly, I have put it into my own pocket, and we are linked by its worn nickel chain. I am used to dipping my hands into his pockets, especially his trousers, for small change. Sometimes I am too drunk or too overwhelmed by disappointment to distinguish between my pockets and his, and our combined unemployment money is spent in an indiscriminate fog between the bakery and the bar.

His father has given up his generous visits, when sausage and ham and pear-shaped cheeses would be our diet for the first five days of each fortnight.

The door needs a hefty shove – not difficult to accomplish with the combined weight of our numbed bodies leaning together and bumping the wood automatically.

The place is stifling and dark, but we feel our way first to his bed, where he slumps fully clothed, and then to mine. I sit there with my head in my hands knowing I cannot untie my shoelaces without a long fumble, and think how we have stopped avoiding walking round that

corner; stopped lurching together a full block further, to where neither of us ever walked with her.

We have also stopped avoiding the bar where we had our fights over her, where I first drew blood from his cheekbone and my knuckles at once.

I can hear his groans across the hall, and suddenly, the scratching of my dog at the front door. I must stagger to let it in. It will lap at the bowl and lie on the front mat until the early afternoon, and then will summon me with the wet nose push it has learnt will startle me into action.

Geffron will grunt scrambled coffee words, and I will slam the pot on the stove, which sees little else. He is more provoked by noise when he wakes, and we have had many disagreements outside the dirty bathroom.

I lean back on my flat pillows in my underwear and think it will be noon before one of us can open the door for the dog. I look out of the window in an unusual struggle to stay awake, and see the street out there starting to crowd with hats, coats and bags and boots, polished boots and brown shoes. I see the soft swinging pace of a sailor, and know it is far too late now to start hoping to see her red coat.

Playing from Memory

Mireille was at the piano when the earthquake struck. Her cardigan fell open so she pushed one of the pearl buttons into a loose buttonhole, when a slight hum left the instrument and vibrated to her ears. The room shook, slightly. The house shook.

Mireille looked at the old yellow keys, and the black key with the cigarette burn she always could find with the middle finger of her left hand. She did up all the buttons, wondering vaguely whether she would ever find time to tighten the buttonholes with some matching cotton yarn.

The chandelier in the hall tinkled, and suddenly, the house was full of music. Louie, upstairs, had turned on the radio. Alarm or curiosity, that was what always roused Louie to action. It stopped as suddenly as it had started.

'An earthquake! Did you feel?' he shouted from the upstairs landing.

Mireille knew that if she did not answer, he would be down, plaguing her with questions, prodding a response out of her with sharp restless fingers.

'Ah!' It was not a real answer. She smiled. It was a noise, neither negative nor affirmative. A noise intended to keep her brother at bay. She looked down at the pearl buttons of the cardigan. If Louie were not there, she would run upstairs to wait for the man Marius in the bedroom.

Perhaps she would throw open the cardigan, lie back on her many blue pillows and wait for him in the half-light coming through the shutters. They would make love while the house shook.

The piano hummed again. Mireille stretched her fingers and played a chord.

Once. Sharply.

'Was that you?' Louie shouted from the stairs.

Mireille answered by playing the opening bars of Für Elise. As she played, the chandelier in the hall accompanied her tinkling on a higher octave. She knew she was afraid. Her skirt had bunched between her knees and her feet were off the pedals now, huddled under the long stool.

Louie entered the room bearing a blue enamel basin full of water. He placed it carefully in the centre of the carpet, where the design formed a circle of blue Fleurs de Lys. 'When the water ripples, you know another tremor is on the way,' he said, eyes small and dark behind metal-framed glasses. 'We can watch the water and know.'

'The piano,' Mireille said ineffectually, picking up her fingers and letting them drop again, creating a loud staccato, which quickly died in the room.

'What?'

'The piano hums just before. And I am waiting for Marius. Take that away. It will ripple just as well in the kitchen.'

'Do you want me to go out?'

'Yes,' she said plainly.

'So you and Marius –' The flat discs of his glasses glinted.

'You know why.'

Louie picked the basin carefully by placing a hand on exactly opposite sides of its circumference, leaving the water almost motionless. Then he tilted it a bit. 'I won't wet the carpet,' he said, before the girl spoke.

Mireille knew he would be gone – out of the windows in the dining room and away through the bushes at the bottom of the garden – in minutes. He had planned and used his many play escape routes during the interminable summers, and the gaps in the hedges widened as he outgrew them and the games.

She stretched her arms on either side of her. Two fingers touched the first and the last keys on the piano. Loose buttonholes released the pearls and the cardigan fell open again. Its light blue cotton tinted her skin slightly so that when she looked down at the hollow between her breasts, it looked milky blue.

When she climbed the stairs to her room, the balustrade shook. The tremor made the wrought iron hum; an audible twang that sang in her head. For a moment, Mireille stood still, one foot not yet touching the landing. Within the grandfather clock in the corner, a vibration was giving out an untimely half-chime.

'I should not be afraid,' she said aloud. Her voice did not echo in the stairwell as usual. Looking up at the ceiling, Mireille saw slight creases of plaster bulge and then crack. She blinked, wondering whether it was her fear, her imagination.

When she looked up again, the ceiling had two fine cracks that ran along a concealed metal beam.

When Marius came, he would enter through the front door, run up the stairs two at a time, keys jingling in his pocket, throw her bedroom door open and spread his arms silently as if to say, Here I am! He would move to the chair with the L-shaped rent in the arm, where he always left his clothes, and undress in the remaining light. He always said evening was the best time of the day. And he always said it then.

Mireille placed a hand on the dull brass knob of the door. It was warm. It had been hot all day, crickets hardly letting off at all. She had taken off her linen dress and bra earlier, putting on an old flowered skirt and the blue cotton cardigan over a pair of white panties.

Barefooted, she sat at the piano for the entire afternoon, playing from memory, letting the cardigan fall open as it may. She looked down at the pearl buttons often. As she did now, entering her dark bedroom on tiptoe, as if careful not to wake herself, as if she were already in bed.

The sheets were still thrown back from the morning. Mireille reached the bed and clung to the white enamel knobs at the end of its dull brass rail. On the dressing table, two scent bottles tinkled faintly against each other, setting a tune on the air. It was stifling.

If this was going to be serious, Louie should not be out at all. Rather than taking off to the village to keep out of their way, her brother should have been kept close to home. They should all get under the great dining room table, perhaps. What was one to do in an earthquake? There was an archway in the cellar, a deep low archway of red brick that wept moisture onto the floor and kept wine bottles dewy. The air down there was humid and almost unbreathable.

Should they all go down there, into the musty smell, to survive the earthquake? Mireille moved to the bathroom and quickly ran some water into the sink. Would it ripple? Did this work as well as a blue basin in the middle of a carpet?

She looked at the mirror, whose corner crack, made years ago when her mother had been in a temper, spread and slit suddenly upward, bisecting the pane neatly in two triangles.

'It's bad.' Her voice was steady but dull in the tiled room. Dry now since her morning shower, its pink and black elaboration reminded her of her mother again. Had she feared earthquakes? Was it like this at any time for her? Did she await a lover while instruments hummed and mirrors cracked around her?

There was a slight rustle behind her and Marius appeared in the mirror. He had not burst in as usual, making her laugh and catch her breath at the same time.

'Surface waves are of many kinds,' he said. 'They are not as clearly separable as body waves. There are two main types – Rayleigh and Love.'

'What are you saying?' She peered at him through the cracked mirror, her eyes wide.

'Reciting from memory. About...'

Mireille looked at him strangely. His hair had blown into his eyes from running up the stairs; his shirt was already unbuttoned to the waist. He looked almost exactly the same as always, but his mouth was in a line, his teeth glinted slightly.

'Seismic activity,' he said softly.

She looked away from the mirror and into his face. 'Marius? Are you afraid?'

'I learned all about earthquakes. But very long ago.' He did not approach her.

'Louie ran water into a basin,' she said flatly. Marius laughed. He threw back his head and his blond hair moved as if in a light wind. In one step, he reached Mireille and drew her close. Holding her away from him after a few seconds, he looked at the unbuttoned cardigan and her skin underneath. His chin touched her hair as she looked down too.

In the bedroom, the scent bottles jingled, then stopped.

'I don't remember the last earthquake,' she said. 'I was too young. Mama was still alive.'

'Come here,' he said.

The sheets were warm. The room was suffocating; slants of yellow light were still visible through the shutter louvres.

Mireille turned to Marius. His eyes were half shut. 'I played all afternoon,' she said softly. 'I played from memory. Czerny. Beethoven. Chopin.' She turned her head away, and looked at the scent bottles, wondering whether she should move them apart, wondering how long Louie would be and whether the village was in panic.

'Should we go to the cellar?' Marius spoke her thoughts.

So he feared the earthquake too. She had an absurd vision of the three of them, huddled under the cellar archway, Marius talking incessantly about seismic waves, Louie's glasses held in his fist and her cardigan hanging open. She wanted to tell him to say more, to speak to her of waves. The word seemed less damaging than shocks.

'Where did you learn about...? '

A door slammed downstairs. She started, then fell back once more. A reverie came over her. This, after all, was not so different from other afternoons. Her eyes closed, and fluttered open again. It was hot, hazy. She was drowsy.

110

Was it Louie's voice that travelled up to where she stood, in the middle of her bedroom, looking at Marius lying in a tangle of white sheets, his head and shoulders resting against a clutch of blue pillows?

It must have been a waking dream, in which her brother shouted, 'Hey, you two! I know you want to be alone and all that, but in the village, they are saying we had better get to an open space.'

In the dream, Louie was breathless. He had run all the way. Speaking from the middle of the stairs, he sounded younger than thirteen, younger than ever. As young as when her mother had sent the hairbrush flying to crack the mirror. He was a young child, grey as a pigeon, glasses reflecting light to make him seem more precocious than ever.

He was a young child, popping his head round the door, pulling it back abruptly when he saw Mireille standing in the middle of the room in her panties.

'It's going to be all right,' she said. Her mouth was tight; she could hardly say the words. It was a dream, after all, she thought.

'It won't get worse than this,' said Marius. So he was awake. Or asleep in the dream with her.

'How do you know?' asked the child, its voice coming subdued and dull around the door. 'How do you know?'

The dream words throbbed through the room, through the house, setting the place a-shiver. Mireille woke suddenly to a shock and tremor.

'Mercalli and Richter!' exclaimed Marius. His eyes glinted in the half-light. His mouth was drawn against his teeth in a slitted smile.

Mireille watched him make a conscious effort to fix the expression on his face.

'Reciting from memory,' she said lightly. 'Are you?' Her thoughts were still blurred. Surely, she had not slept deeply enough to dream. She listened. The world seemed quieter than ever. Birds had stopped chirping outside the windows. She pulled on the blue cardigan, fiddling with the buttonholes again. Marius did not say anything as she left the room. Past the grandfather clock, under the chandelier that had stopped its tinkling, Mireille padded in bare feet.

When she got to the piano and sat down, she listened for longer than a minute for a vibrating hum in its deep belly. None came. Her fingers flexed and automatically, she spaced her fingers to play C. The chord was not played. Mireille kept her fingers suspended over the keys. It was too dark now to see the cigarette burn on the black key. The room had cooled only slightly.

From a distance, a low rumbling seemed to come from the direction of the village.

'What was that?' she thought aloud.

'I told you,' said Marius from the door. 'It's not going to get worse.' He moved up to her until he touched her shoulders with his side. Firm fingers circled her wrist.

'Do you remember Mama?' she asked, even though she knew he did not. 'Was she afraid of earthquakes?'

'You said you were twelve when she died.'

'And Louie was six. But was she afraid, do you think?' Mireille wrapped the fronts of the cardigan around her.

'Can you recite from memory?' he asked, after they had listened to the absence of outside noises for a while.

'What?'

'Anything. Poetry.'

Mireille shook her head in the dark, feeling her lover's form slide closer on the edge of the piano stool, comparing him with Louie, whose slight body was always cool, and the way he prodded her with thin fingers for attention.

'I can only remember chords and notes by heart,' she admitted.

'Then play something from memory.' He stopped talking. The sudden hum from the belly of the piano was not loud, but Marius looked scared.

'Like ripples in water...' she said. She should have asked Louie to stay in the house with them. It was no time for him to be roaming the village. But he was not a tiny child anymore, not like she had imagined him that afternoon, pale and sagely pensive, like a baby owl.

When the house shook, groans and creaks from masonry and furniture sounded around them. Mireille struck the keys suddenly. The tune spun out from her fingertips and filled the house. It was bizarre, crazy. She played for what felt like a long time, loudly, until the tremor ceased, and tinkling from the chandelier in the hall diminished in the silence she left in the air after the last chord.

The man shifted on the seat beside her.

'I think that was the last of it.'

Marius's head turned suddenly. 'There are people in the garden.'

Mireille spun round, clutching the sides of the cardigan close around her. Voices carried up to her as she ran up the stairs. As she dressed, she could hear panicked voices fill the space around the piano. From the grandfather clock on the stairs came another chime, this

114

time accurately on the hour. Soon it would be night. Someone had turned on the light downstairs. Everything was yellow with it.

She descended the stairs, cautiously, as if she knew who the visitors were, as if she knew what she had to confront. Her afternoon dream could no longer be summoned. There was no child in glasses popping a small head around a door. Her brother was stretched out on the sofa, green brocade paling his skin, making him look pigeon grey.

'Falling debris...' Marius started to say. He looked in alarm at her eyes, the widening and stretching of her silent lips. 'Don't cry. Yes, c-come here, cry.' Confusion made him stammer.

Mireille avoided his open arms and approached the sofa. 'Where are his glasses?'

One of the village women wept suffocatingly into a handful of checked kerchief. Mireille regarded her strangely. She stood over Louie and placed a finger on a stray lock of hair on his forehead. 'He is dead, isn't he?

He died when we were up there. And I played the piano.' She looked at Marius. 'We should have crept under the great arch in the cellar... the three of us, together.'

They watched as she sat in front of the piano, and touched the key with the cigarette burn in it. She poised her hands to play a chord, but it never came. In the kitchen, the water in the blue enamel basin was still and un-rippled, but the piano keys were splashed with tears.

Cacti

There was a huge *Ferocactus latispinus* in a great terracotta pot in the corner. Marianna stood and looked at it for a long time. A green *Not for Sale* sticker hung from a thin string drawn tightly round the pot. The cactus needed potting up – it had outgrown the container and Marianna imagined how she would tackle the job. The curving flat red spines were formidable, those closest to the window gleaming with a metallic rusty glow. It was a magnificent specimen. She wished she could rotate the pot to see the part of the globular trunk that faced the corner of the glasshouse, to see if it were as perfect as the section she could see. The grey-green flesh was unspotted, unblemished and plump. Someone who understood cacti had cared for it for years.

The *Not for Sale* ticket swung a little as someone came through the glasshouse door and let in a slight draught, but Marianna did not look round. She did the round of the Cacti and Succulents section again, examining each plant in its green plastic or clay pot; straining on tiptoe for the top shelves, or bending breathlessly to see the lower ones. The larger specimens were ranged on the furthest shelf – the last stagger of tiers that ringed the inside of the house, their huge pots stained white in places. Some were chalked 'Not for Sale' and had no string or ticket. Most small pots had price tags.

There was a magnificent *Oreocereus celsianus*, its soft white hairs trailing upwards and out, not hiding the gold spines underneath. Marianna would have loved to pick it up and take it home, but the plastic tag stuck like a gravestone into the chipped gravel round the cactus base was scrawled brightly with a price in purple felt pen. Thirteen dollars. She looked past it at a range of smaller pots, the two year old ones. She could gauge their age easily, even the vigorous growers that dwarfed the rest. A *Cereus peruvianis*, lanky and solitary and unbranched, towered over some other pots. Its short barbs were grouped in clumps of seven. Without counting Marianna knew they were seven, and that since her last visit the tall cactus had grown another few centimetres. When it hit the top of the greenhouse it would be time for action to be taken, and she imagined what she would do to the tall plant; how she would slice it gently and dry the wound out carefully for a week until it was time to replant the cutting and watch the stump for offsets. All in her mind, she saw how she would count the tiny sprouts as they appeared round the base of the old stump, and how she would re-pot them in a few weeks.

The Ferocactus caught her eye again. It flowered three times since she had known it: a huge white bloom almost sexual in its grandeur. Every time it happened Marianna visited the nursery daily until the flower wilted and died, its glory over.

The *Notocactus ottonis* bloomed at night, and she could only see the dying yellow funnels the next morning, knowing the part inside she could not see was a delicate light green. She hoped her surreptitious guilty look was not seen by the nurseryman. She could not be there at night; the nursery was shut and barred at sundown, and often she was the last to pass the gate, the nurseryman giving her familiar figure a curious look as she sidled past him silently. She imagined it had been his hand that scrawled the thick purple 'Not For Sale' on the tickets, his hand that turned pots gently to catch the spring sunlight evenly after the inactivity of the long winter; his hand that removed withered and blackened flowers when they were dead, or added a fine pebbly top-dressing to the pots.

She thought of his tough callused hands tenderly re-potting spiny plants without need for gloves; thick garden hands that needed no protection against the needles; white, red or golden. She imagined the glochids of the *Opuntia splendens* that glanced his tanned skin, not even clinging for an instant but slipping past – with her they would cling and prick and sting, under her nails and between her fingers, if she dared to brush the pads of that cactus with bare skin. She wondered how he would handle the *Mammillaria perbella* when it was its turn to be placed in a larger pot, how he would cup the little decorative sphere with its white and pink thorny

119

spines in the inside of his upturned hand, carefully cradle it until he coaxed it into the bed of mixture, and then how he would press the earth round its base, covering its roots carefully for another season. Gently.

Ignoring the Lithops, which she privately detested, Marianna walked past the Kalanchoes clustered together, with their pink flower bells already opening, and looked for the Haworthias, which had been moved. She never paused there long, because the clumpy tentacle-like plants were only vaguely interesting to her, and moved on to the Euphorbias. Grouped together in an odd assortment of differently sized pots they presented a jumbled vision, and it was with some effort she kept her hands tightly clenched. She wanted to move them, sort them out and arrange them; examine the *horrida* most of all, because it had long menacing needles that belied the peaceful green of its trunk. Already, red bracts were present: soon they would open. The year had flown past and she remembered last year's Euphorbias and how the nurseryman had neglected them too, pushing them together into a lower corner in the house, probably glad to see them sold. There were no Euphorbias with Not For Sale signs.

The hanging Rhipsalidopsis and Schlumbergeras swung above her head, but she did not look up. She knew they were there, too many of them: they were too popular. Every year the nursery received consignment upon consignment from Victoria and they would all sell, leaving her favourite old ones behind.

The *Cleistocactus straussii* in the corner was close to twenty years old; she did not dare verify this with the man. He shuffled somewhere behind her, and although she knew he was used to her almost constant presence in the Cacti and Succulents section, he must have been curious about her fixation and dedication. Perhaps he wondered how she found so much time to spend getting in his way. They had never said a word to each other; she had never bought a thing, and she thought he could sense her eyes on his hands as he moved pots, poured diluted fertiliser, stacked trays. She watched him sell the larger cacti; then her eyes would follow the purchasers until they disappeared from sight. She avoided looking at the empty place on the shelf, and stood aside, trying to remember the name of the piece of music that drifted in every time the door was opened, until he came and filled it with another potted cactus, moved remaining pots to hide the gap.

Now she peered at the plump *Gymnocalycium denudatum* perched on the highest shelf in a squat pot. Her back chastised him for placing it so high. The plant was hardly visible; round and stubby green and red spheres embedded in the soil. She felt him resolve to move the pot to below eye level when she moved out of the way.

She did not move. The strains of some music she had never heard before came through the greenhouse door that thudded again, as if to announce some strange adagio. It was Schubert. No – this was like nothing she was familiar with. But it would not distract her from what she wanted to see. Marianna peered high, standing on her toes to look again at the Rebutias that would flower in a week. These tiny globes were among her favourites. She knew she puzzled him with her resistance to buy. Was the music some sort of new inducement? She would ignore it then – disregard the diminishing chords she heard in a coda that was flat and abrupt. She spent hours in his nursery staring at the cacti, her fascination apparent. Why he never spoke to her was another mystery; perhaps one he never addressed. Perhaps he thought music was a form of persuasion. Or dismissal.

She moved again to the Ferocactus, its size and age never failing to captivate her. She longed to turn the pot to look at its blind side. On either flank were two identical pots of

Borzicactus aureispinus, obviously put there by the nurseryman for effect and contrast. Their spines were deceptively soft-looking and golden, trunks long and slender and a beautiful light green. They crowded and clustered and emphasised the spatulate red thorns of the Ferocactus.

122

It was nearly time to leave. She strained to hear the music, but it must have been turned off ages ago. He was making obvious noises behind her. A half-formed resolve flitted into her mind, but she shrugged it off in panic. She thought again of his weathered but sensuous hands as they cradled the Mammillaria and a pink blush rose to her cheeks. Then she quickly brushed past him on her way out. Her throat tightened.

'The Ferocactus needs rotating,' she whispered as she went by.

Allegro Ma Non Troppo

Was it wrong to suppose that – since she had seen the small bust of the composer on his piano – that Anselm liked Schubert?

Anselm: what a name. She met him at the flea market, looking through old sheet music. At first she was annoyed, and then curious.

'I like the ones that have been annotated in pencil.' He had spoken in a grave way to her, pointing to a score with words in the margin.

Marlene liked the way he looked at her immediately, and was surprised they sought exactly the same thing. She liked to find stained sheets of music with dark or faint marks in a handwriting that spoke of the turn of the century: the turn of the eighteenth and nineteenth centuries, that is. Writing then was almost artistic. People wrote with care, with flourishes, with dignity and poise, she liked to think, feeling terribly romantic. And that in essence was what she wanted: romance: the old-fashioned romantic feeling that ancient- looking music sheets aroused in her.

'You see…' The man continued, his hair in his eyes and gold-rimmed glasses glinting in the sun. 'I can tell or feel how the musician interpreted the music. Sometimes I am lucky enough to find pages belonging to a conductor!'

'Really!' Marlene wondered why he bothered telling her all this.

Coincidences were not something Marlene believed in, yet they happened, and happened to her. She treated them lightly or ignored them altogether; disregarded the scientific regard of coincidences that her friend Poppy termed 'convergence'.

Scientists, Poppy said often and rather seriously, regarded random coincidental events as necessary and even vital: they were what provoked the shifts that evolved organisms, to take the shapes and behaviours we know. Marlene always laughed at her friend's serious and studied ways, being the least scientific of creatures; and a cynic on top of that. She asked Poppy – meaning to irritate her out of her pedantic mood – if there was any romance in biology.

The reply was given promptly, gravely, with Poppy's fixed gaze, her beautiful green eyes steady: the picture of patience. 'Of course, Marlene. Of *course* there is romance in science.'

And this was perhaps what she meant: a chance event that proved to be momentous. The random meeting of two like-minded individuals at a flea market: meeting another whose search coincided almost exactly with her own. She had naturally forgotten what Poppy added to her answer. It was long and involved, making Marlene lose interest and start to look away. She was certainly not thinking of anything scientific when she met Anselm, and although it was yet another coincidence – or perhaps not such a great one, considering their quest – when they met at another market on the following Sunday, she was pleased rather than perplexed. And so, if his smile was anything to go by, was Anselm.

So pleased was he that he asked her to an outdoor café for a late breakfast, where they talked little about sheet music, or composers, or handwriting. Neither did they talk about scientific convergence: but coincidences did enter the conversation once or twice. It was light-hearted and entertaining; each talked unselfconsciously about what they did and what they read, and Marlene enjoyed it more than anything she had done in recent months, perhaps years.

She had to tell Poppy about this madly handsome man whose passion for sheet music almost matched her own. She had to tell her about his brilliant eyes and his metallic spectacles that slid repeatedly to the end of his nose so that he generally looked over the top of them at her, rather than through them. His teeth were charmingly uneven but his smile frequent and straight, suggesting an intelligent mind that matched – in a way – his long sensitive fingers she imagined travelling easily over a piano keyboard.

What they talked about most that morning at the market café was food.

'One day, in my search for Sibelius, or at the very least Schoenberg, I came across a thin green book that was annotated in pencil in a rather strange way, for its age.' He crumbled the corner of a croissant and looked around for more butter.

'Oh yes?'

'Yes, Marlene.' He said her name so matter-of-factly and clearly it made her blink. 'It was sloping to the left, to suggest the writer was left-handed. Not a very common thing, since left-handedness was discouraged until the mid-1900s. It was a rounded hand, and there were many deletions … erasures … as if the person was very unsure of herself.'

'Then it was a woman.'

'Oh – I don't really *know*.' He put down his knife and looked at her, tilting his head as if to say how perfectly right, to question one's immediate decision about anything one found.

He described the recipes in the book, a Viennese book that even from its ingredients smacked of the Austro-Hungarian Empire: how they indicated that family life, eating habits and also the very things people ate, had changed since the seventeen and eighteen hundreds. The recipe names were all in German, he said: subtitled in capital letters in English, with the method of preparation given in long complete sentences that were so elaborate as to be almost literary.

Marlene imagined the book clearly because of his minute narrative, liking the way he described thumb marks that spoke of cream, beef dripping, and thick yellow butter. Real chicken stock, suet, liver, nutmeg and sweet Hungarian paprika: things she rarely or never used.

The next time they met it was by arrangement, not coincidence. And Poppy was told on the phone that Marlene was about to see this Anselm again.

'Is it wise?' Poppy's telephone voice was even more serious than when heard live.

'I cannot weigh him or measure him,' said Marlene with a laugh, mocking her scientist friend. 'So I cannot gauge at all what he is really like. But I'd like to find out. It might be exciting.'

'I think you are already excited.' Poppy made the accusation sound like a scientific observation.

And of course she was.

'And don't forget what I told you the other day about causation… um, motivation.'

Marlene could not remember at all what Poppy had said. 'Of course not.' She pulled a grimace.

And it certainly had been fun and exciting looking for music together up in the hills, where they had lunch at a pub and talked about food again. Anselm was in an up-beat mood, humming bits out of something Marlene could not name, although she recognised the tune.

'You don't play Schubert, then.' He smiled. It was a test.

'Um – no! I don't play at all. Do you?'

'Yes.' Then he shook his head. 'You *sing* then.'

And Marlene nodded, not wanting to say anything to jeopardise this delightful beginning of something she wanted to pursue. Not wanting to say she only sang when she was absolutely sure she was alone: such as at the steering wheel in slow traffic, cheering herself up on the way somewhere: yodelling at the top of her voice in a closed car and collapsing in private giggles when she found someone watching from another vehicle.

They found something together that day. It was starting to cloud over and the skies threatened rain. They had decided to go on to Anselm's house, and it looked very much as if they would have to make an earlier start than planned. But the little blue book seemed interesting, and they both touched it at once, lifting it together out of a crammed banana box so that it was unclear who had seen it first.

Marlene dismissed it, but knew Poppy would have said it was one of those tiny coincidences that had a micro effect on life. A minute random event that could shift everything that happened afterwards, making things diverge … or converge.

'Hey!' Anselm obviously recognized what they held jointly with almost-touching hands. 'This is… Hey – do you see what this is?'

'A life of Salieri.' Marelene read the frontispiece as he gently thumbed open the pages.

'Mm – more than that. This guy, this biographer, claims to have discovered some new details about Salieri and Mozart – here, let me see.' He turned, holding the book, and started to pore through the pages. 'Ha!' He exclaimed and mumbled as he read. 'The usual mention of Schubert… Legnano, Vienna – yes.' Every now and then, he turned a page toward Marlene, so she could see a portrait, the picture of a house, a group of men in tailcoats and wigs, a female portrait. Anselm said nothing more for a long while, so she did not utter a word.

'Do you want this?'

'No,' she laughed. 'You do!'

'I mean…'

She laughed again at the transparent look of desire and hope – hope she did not want it as badly – on his face.

At his house, which had beautiful French windows where her reflection seemed repeated too many times, and where her plain straight blonde hair and grey eyes seemed to become suddenly commonplace, she took in the rosewood upright piano in a corner, and rows of glazed bookcases whose panes also reflected the way she stood; her thin shoulders, how her legs seemed all of a sudden to be knock-kneed.

I am becoming self-conscious, she thought, and quickly turned away from herself, only to see Anselm too was dragging his eyes from his own reflected form: sectioned neatly from blonde head to turned-out toes, in the spotless French windowpanes. So he too was self-conscious, wanting to make a better impression than his appearance allowed him. Another coincidence? She thought of what Poppy's scientific analysis of this encounter would be and smiled.

On a table cluttered with the paraphernalia of the random collector of found objects, she counted six libretti, a biography of Arrigo Boito – a name not entirely mysterious to her – an ancient looking metronome, and a conductor's baton.

She had to sigh in recognition. The way the things were grouped suggested they were displayed, but not very artistically. She had an eye for that sort of thing: a flair on which she set much store, something she was proud of, not being really sure whether she had any other talents. The little obsidian bust she spied on top the piano, for example, would have made the whole display look much more elaborate, adding height, substance and contrast.

'The way you have done this…' She looked up and started to offer her thoughts, but Anselm was taking out a score, making her look at the elegant writing in the margins and on top of some of the notes.

'*Allegro, ma non troppo,*' he said, a delicate finger underlining the faint words pencilled goodness knew how long ago. 'Cheerful, but not overly!' He made it sound like a joke rather than a loose translation.

Later, when he had shown her the garden and the way he had styled the back veranda so that it resembled a balustraded limestone terrace such as one would find in Italy or France, she almost forgot about the display on the table.

'That small black bust,' she said, 'it's obsidian, isn't it?'

There was a hint of pleasure in his smile. 'Yes – most people think it's onyx. And it's Schubert, of course. I'll tell you how I got it…' His tone suggested happy conspiracy rather than condescending pedantry.

He thinks I know what he knows, thought Marlene. She knew Poppy put a great deal of importance on compatibility. And to a certain extent, she saw its significance herself: what was the use of investing time, interest and hope in someone who would eventually drift off to someone else; someone who liked the same things they did?

So was it wrong to suppose he liked Schubert, seeing he owned a beautiful little bust of the composer, and seemed very willing to launch a conversation about him? Marlene wondered about this, and about Anselm – the way he talked to her, the way he suggested they had more in common than she secretly supposed, the way he stopped and turned to look at her in silence whenever he put on some music he thought she would recognise – and started to feel not altogether like a fraud, because she knew he suspected she was not the musician he had thought. And not altogether like an equal, because she knew now he was her intellectual superior. But not altogether a disparate soul: there was something there they shared. Wasn't there?

One weekend later on, alone and happy to be so, she combed the Valley open-air markets, raking through boxes of old books, lifting figurines and small pieces of pottery, as if she could gauge their worth from their weight. She was looking – as usual – for flat items, such as music scores, maps, old lace handkerchiefs. She sought pressed flowers, concert programmes, and dance cards from long-ago balls. What she would prize above all was a net reticule, a small pair of gloves... Ah! She lifted a slender ivory case from a table, knowing very well, if she were very lucky, that inside would be a fine lady's fan, hopefully still bearing its tassel and perfect accordion pleats. Yes – it was creamy white, to match the case, made of something like Belgian or Spanish lace.

'I'll take it.' She did not really stop to haggle, and reached for her wallet. That was when she saw the red book. Its cover was damaged, but its size was attractive, with not more than about ten dozen pages and suggesting a readership – in its day – of either strict connoisseurs or easy to bore dabblers. She was not sure. But it was a biography of Franz Schubert, and the dancing words on the page arrested her. Obviously part of a series: 'The Great Musicians', there was a list at the back that included a dozen or so other composers. A series edited by Francis Hueffer, she read, thinking at once of Anselm, and how he would know. He would be sure to state, even before he read the words, that this particular book was written by H F Frost. The thought made her smile. The book had just over a hundred small pages, plus a short chronology of Schubert's works. It was not particularly well set out – there were no chapters, no pictures, and no proper index: merely a short table of contents, which offended her sense of order, her sense of design.

'And this, as well,' she said to the wispy man who ran the stall. He was already handing out change, but did not seem nonplussed to have another object thrust at him. This was common market behaviour – people made impulsive purchases, changed their minds, haggled.

Clutching her crumpled brown paper bag, she hurried home, wishing she was on familiar enough terms with Anselm to drop in on him unannounced, to thrust the book at him without a word, with a smile a little different to the one she had given the stallholder. But she had to wait until she got an invitation, which was Poppy's advice. Advice well intended, to be sure, but with which she was becoming increasingly impatient.

So it was at a small restaurant – where Anselm said they could get real *Kalbshaxen*, with the sauce served separately, and authentic potato dumplings – that she decided to proffer her small gift.

'Is it really wise?' Poppy had asked her usual polite but pointed question, and looked at the small red book, raising a scientific eyebrow. 'This looks like a ... an *intimate* gift. What's your real motivation here, Marlene?'

'Motivation? Poppy, we are friends. I know he likes Schubert – I just picked up something I think he'd appreciate. What motivation?'

But Marlene understood the question – knew the answer. It was that she did not want to address her friend's ponderous analysis of what she could possibly want from her friendship with Anselm. Perhaps if they embraced, if he kissed her, perhaps … when they slept together, it would be time to face such questions. But now? Now she wanted to see his face when he opened the little parcel.

He opened it, put his knife down and exclaimed. 'Oh!' He looked closely, through those metal spectacles, at the flat packet. 'Is it my birthday?'

Marlene laughed.

Anselm laughed.

'I don't know when your birthday is,' she said, nervous now, and wanting him to hurry up and diffuse the suspense.

'November,' he said. 'Months away. But this is fabulous. An un-birthday present. How super.' Genuine pleasure lit up his eyes. His glasses slid down his nose and he looked at her over them. 'Thank you.'

'Open it.'

'Oh – oh wow, the Frost book.'

'You have it – you know it.' Marlene was disappointed.

'I have two! It's a fascinating book to read, not so much because it contains anything new, but because it gives an interesting insight to the state of Schubert research just over a hundred years ago. What they had discovered, and under what premises they laboured then.'

Marlene sighed with a kind of relief. He liked it. His knowledge, though, made her breathless, unsure of herself: she somehow felt just a touch mediocre, in comparison.

'You knew this, didn't you?' He asked a dozen questions at once. 'You know I love this, don't you? Where did you *find* this? It contains lots of quaint Victorian language, you know. Did you read it before you packed it so nicely? It's got all these politically incorrect remarks – never could have been released today. And it's inaccurate with names and things, in places – a gem of a book.'

They looked down at it together. Marlene sipped wine, in two minds about her gift – was Poppy right?

But Anselm went on about the book. He speared a piece of veal after pouring its thick sauce – which arrived in an ordinary stainless steel gravy boat – over it. He was enjoying the meal, the whole evening, enormously. It showed on his face, in his eyes, whose spectacles seemed both superfluous and necessary: on his faintly reddened cheeks. 'Chronologically speaking, this biography appeared just a few years after Grove's famous article in his dictionary.'

Marlene did not ask who Grove was.

'Back then, as you very well know, Marlene, many things we take for granted now were simply not known. Many of Schubert's works were yet to be published, the great C Major Symphony was still thought to date from 1828!'

Marlene hazarded a contribution. 'There were no CD numbers.'

'Exactly! No Deutsch numbers!' Anselm exclaimed in happy conspiracy. He lifted his glass to her. 'Isn't this veal absolutely delicious?'

She had to agree. She had noticed the parsnips and carrots were diced haphazardly, in totally random shapes, which she liked. It looked like a real homemade dish, prepared lovingly by some avid Viennese cook, rather than by a cleverly coached chef with a comprehensive – but artificial – understanding of food and eating.

'Now...' Anselm raised a finger. 'After this, for which I thank you...' He rose slightly from his seat, leaned over and kissed Marlene on the cheek. Although chaste and brief, it was warm and full of suggestion. Her skin tingled. She blushed, and was too late to kiss him back, as he sat back promptly in his chair.

'… After this,' he continued, 'I hope you will ask me up for coffee and show me your collection of sheet music!'

Marlene had a suspicion this might happen, and was pleased she had tidied up and put together a few of her best pieces. 'I don't have much left,' she admitted.

'Left? Are you a dealer – is that what you are? I have wondered and wondered what it is you do with your scores, since you do not play.'

Marlene's pulse quickened when he repeated 'wondered'. He thought about her. She started to tell him about her pieces. 'I take some of the most beautiful pages…'

But the waiter was there, whipping away the empty bottle of wine and suggesting *Gugelhupf* for dessert.

'Oh – I couldn't possibly.' She held a hand to her waist.

'Oh, come on – be a devil. Let's share a slice,' said Anselm, prompting a new intimacy that would put the evening definitely on a course along which she was wondering about steering.

'What is so *special* about your little book, Marlene, is something you probably do not know.' He said this in a tone that belied his words. Of course she knew, his voice said. Of course she had read everything about Schubert.

139

'It contains a rare introduction that neither of my editions contain. Your find is priceless – for me, at any rate!'

'Oh, how wonderful,' she said. 'When you said you had two, I thought I'd come up with something – um…'

'Redundant? No. No!' He laughed, as if she had made a very intelligent remark. 'Come on – it is not every day one runs into a Frost biography.'

'No,' she agreed.

Her flat was spotless. She looked at it through his eyes, noting with dismay the ordinary furniture that was neither antique nor new, and the colour of the walls, which seemed tonight to be overdone.

'I cannot give you Viennese coffee,' she said, a bit nervous to have him in her domain, her territory.

Anselm shook his head. 'That recipe book – do you remember it? Do you remember the time we …?'

She nodded.

'It has four blank pages at the back that a different person has filled with extra recipes. They are mainly Hungarian, and the writing slants to the right, very finely, in ink. Do you know what *Rigó Jansci* is?'

Marlene's heart sank. She knew then it would always be that way: his assumptions about her knowledge of things would always intrude. His presumptions of whatever overlap he thought they had would eventually bring about a huge disappointment she would have to do something about, before it escalated and ruined everything. 'No,' she said flatly.

'Neither did I. I managed to translate a few words and it turns out it's filled and iced slices of chocolate cake, which would certainly take over a day to make.' He wandered over to a square table that Marlene had covered with a beige silk shawl whose deep fringe disguised its humble design. On it, she had placed a folio of music, her new ivory lace fan and a collection of pressed flowers mounted on oval disks. Anselm picked up the folio, whose black cover, stained peeling label and reinforced corners must have been entirely familiar in his hands: she had seen many like it in his house. Opening it, he leaved forward and back until he found something he recognised.

For a while, there was silence as he pored over the notes.

'More Schubert,' he mumbled, and hummed. 'I knew you'd like this scherzo.'

'You know – I have never heard you play,' she said quietly. Somehow she knew that that too, he would do splendidly, sitting at his upright piano, fingering the keys with familiarity laced with talent.

Anselm laughed. 'One day you will,' he said, with confidence. 'Now – before coffee, after coffee, show me

141

what it is you do with your scores.' He placed the folio in the exact spot from where he lifted it and to Marlene's utter surprise, took her in his arms. His kiss was sudden, but there was nothing violent or impetuous about it. Slowly and deliberately, his mouth captured hers, and for a long instant they were joined not only physically – his arms around her and her hands clasped together at his chest – but also somehow mentally. For that split second, Marlene thought she felt him stop thinking.

'Look,' she whispered, when he stepped back and was pushing his glasses up. 'I mean – yes, I'll show you.'

He sought her eyes, his own full of a kind of warm suggestion she was both delighted in and afraid of, wanting above everything else – anything else – for them to find in common everything that was necessary and vital.

She took him to her office or studio – she still had not decided what to call the room – and pointed to a stack of frames that leaned against a wall near a large worktable. 'I take romantic objects, such as sheets of music, old menus, gloves… I found a lovely fan the other week. I put them in compatible groups, and I frame them. They sell very well.'

'Oh!' Anselm's disappointment was palpable. The room was quiet. He had nothing to say. For lack of words, he strode to the stack of frames and walked his fingers over their tops, leafing through the whole collection. 'Oh,' he said again. It was obvious from his silence that what Marlene regarded as her only talent was not to his liking. He thought they had something in common and it turned out they did not.

'So you don't sing.' His voice was flat.

Marlene could not figure his tone. That he was disappointed was certain. 'No – I am not musical at all. I am so sorry to disappoint you. All this time you... I...'

'Yes,' he said. He left the frames exactly as he had found them. 'You actually take the scores apart? I find that um... curious.'

'You find it a pity and a shame and a waste that I don't seem to see their significance.' Marlene's voice was angry – but with herself, not with him. Now she saw what Poppy meant by motivation. She sought the same objects – more or less – as Anselm, but her motivation was entirely different. 'You thought we were similar creatures, but it turns out we are not.'

'Hey – don't take it so seriously!' Anselm crossed the room, took her by the arm and steered her out of the studio, turning out the light as they left. 'I'm surprised, that's all. After all, it *is* a coincidence that we both look for the same thing.'

'I have a friend who has a way of looking at coincidences...' Marlene was close to tears. Her disappointment, too, seemed greater than his.

'What?'

143

Marlene rambled on, not knowing whether to stop talking or to attempt to talk through the embarrassment and hopelessness she felt. 'She's a scientist, my friend Poppy, who talks about convergence and divergence and minute shifts that can change things into others that are entirely different. Over time, that is.'

'I have a similar friend – where's the coffee?' asked Anselm. He made himself at home in her kitchen, looking for mugs and putting the kettle on.

Rather than feeling invaded, rather than a sense of intrusion, Marlene felt reassured. A sudden flood of relief made her wilt.

But Anselm went on about his friend. 'Isn't that a coincidence – Roger talks incessantly about things like that. Things I hardly even give a fleeting thought to he considers absolutely vital. Causation, diversification, and something he calls *mutual affinities of organic beings*. We should introduce them!'

He said *we* – it was not finished. Not over. Marlene exhaled.

'Do you have any real sugar, or must I put one of these things in my coffee?' Anselm smiled and shook a tiny container of saccharine.

'You are not appalled at what I do with sheet music?' Marlene had to know.

Anselm looked up, gazed at her over his glasses. His eyebrows rose. 'I am *allegro*,' he said with a wry smile, '*ma non troppo*. It's okay, I suppose – but I'm not overjoyed.' He sighed, looked down, and then looked at the ceiling. 'Look – different people like different things. I've seen vases covered in postage stamps and boxes decorated with shells...' He saw her face fall. '... and although I don't say your pictures or collages are anything similar, I have an open mind about things like this. The world is big enough to accommodate all of us.'

'You don't think they are awful?'

He shook his head. 'Not awful – just not exactly what I was expecting!'

Marlene looked at her shoes. 'No.' Then she looked up. 'I've misled you, but not intentionally. I first thought we had something in common, that we – you know, that we shared something.'

'Hm.'

'And now I think how things really are – how you actually know about music and actually play the piano and...'

'Oh – just *wait* till you hear me play!' he said.

Marlene tilted her head.

'I'm terrible.'

'I'm sure you're not.'

He laughed. 'No – it's the truth. I do not play well at all, but enjoy it enormously, and I get a lot out of it. And besides, I collect old scores, so it's nice to be able to actually use them sometimes.'

145

'Sometimes? I thought you played professionally.'

'Mm – percussion – and we have printed scores, computer generated.'

He approached her around the small kitchen table and once more, drew her into his arms. 'Did your scientist friend tell you more about coincidences and convergence and divergence?' His kiss was firm and loving.

'Like what?' replied Marlene, after taking a breath.

'That sometimes, coincidentally or not, creatures break the rules and intentionally change things, or keep things the same.' He kissed her again.

'Really?'

Anselm laughed. 'Oh – I don't know if that's a scientific fact, but people *do*. I do. I don't think we should change a thing – do you?'

There was no real necessity to answer.

Encore

Face buried in the bouquet, senses piqued by the sharp jonquil scent, eyes blinded by spotlights and dianthus, she turned to the wings and smiled, then once more looked at the audience. The roar of applause rose and fell, some shouted 'More!' from the back. A few in the stalls rose to their feet, still clapping.

'One more, Moira!' Al Kramer spoke from the wings. He clapped too, but the smile stretched the stitched skin on his chin.

His eyes were dark hollows from where she stood. The spotlights blinded her. She shook her head; another encore would take too long. The evening would tire them all out. But Al nodded, vigorously. 'Play again, play more.' His lips said the words she could not hear. Someone came and took the bouquet. The audience settled. Silence fell in the auditorium. Her accompanist searched her face for a signal. What would she do?

Moira gave the slightest nod, and Carmen moved to the piano, which made the audience erupt once more into encouraging applause. She could decipher now, after so many years, between applause that said a number of things.

"That was wonderful!"

"Play more."

And also "It's late. We've had enough."

147

She held up three fingers to Carmen at the piano, and watched her seek the piece among the sheets they had so quickly put together in some desired sequence, two days ago. When they tried to salvage the tour: after the accident. Before everything else.

Moira took up the clarinet. She loved its weight, knew its feel in her hands. The instrument balanced on her thumb naturally, as if she was born with a place there, on her thumb, for a clarinet to rest.

Before she could inhale softly to give Carmen her cue, she took a brief moment, and looked out over the audience. Spotlights threw all into a darkness in which she could not distinguish faces, but there was no real need to. They all knew her: she was Moira Kramer, her name was on the program. The concert hall organizers had put a poster with her picture and her name in large sloping letters outside. It was done quickly – but it was done well. And she? She did not know a single one of them out there. Perhaps a couple of acquaintances, but an audience was always a crowd of perfect strangers. Strangers who knew her pieces backwards, who understood the nuances and clapped, clapped louder even when confidence ebbed.

She inhaled and Carmen started the introduction, one she knew so well she had to listen hard, lest she miss her place. There was no real danger of that: Carmen was the kind of accompanist who sensed things before they happened, and made way for 'the star of the show', as she always half-seriously called Moira when they practised. No irony or envy in her words. No: Carmen loved her role and fulfilled it perfectly.

Someone applauded longer than the rest. Just a few claps more. It was Al. She looked to where he stood in the wings, and missed the chord. She inhaled again, this time from panic, or exhaustion, or defeat; but Carmen did not miss a beat and came round again, so she raised the reed to her mouth, tongued it, and entered into the chord seamlessly. She had to put Al out of her mind … everything out of her mind, to play this last encore. Then they could go home. They would all clap again, but they would let her go home.

It was a mistake. The Rimsky-Korsakov concerto was a mistake. She should never have raised three fingers at Carmen. Playing this always had her long for the band, not the meagre tinkling of a piano, no matter how ably played, no matter how haunting and emotive. What was Lewis thinking? Carmen could never replace the full power of a wind band behind her, the surge of the rank and file clarinets; the throb of the almost undiscernible trombone solo. No one noticed it but her. Only she noticed the trombone.

She could not allow a tear come to her eye now, not in the middle of this. She would have to cut it short. Short? At such an important concert, it would be suicide.

It would be in the paper the next day: a Friday charity concert – no, Saturday this time – at the most beautiful historic concert hall in town, and she blew the last encore. She could never let it happen. Yet she missed the next entry and Carmen slowed and came back again, without looking at her even once. The piano player would ascribe her misses to excitement, or to tiredness, never to the thoughts she had of trombones. Carmen would never guess why she was being so emotional tonight. If there had been a band behind her, it would be missing one trombone.

It was a long boring drive to Collarbone Creek. All the instruments were in the special trailer the van towed, and their overnight bags were in the back of the van, lumped together. Green leather, red vinyl, and the checked duffel bag Al had carted around since university.

Carmen, the only one without an instrument to worry about, was always first to board.

People knew Moira and Al always sat together, and their instrument cases were always placed side by side in the trailer: a square clarinet case that fitted almost any available space, and his big battered trombone case and its clichéd travel stickers, collected in his funny adolescent way, at every location.

The drive down was uneventful, and the gig went well, except for one minor discord between the first violin and their director, Lewis Wilmarley, who for the first time that season, showed his teeth. It was getting to all of them, at last: the weather, the long drives, the interminable rehearsals and Lewis's perfectionism. But who, of all people, had cause to desire perfection more than Lewis?

Moira knew why the van rolled. Perhaps they all knew. Coming round the steep side of the foothills, the driver changed gear for a steep descent as the sun set ahead of them, sending white shafts of light out of an orange sky to make them all squint and look away. The driver looked in the mirror, and what he saw made him stare and smirk.

Al saw, and looked back, and what he saw made him blanch.

Moira wondered how they all got out of it with nothing but bruises and scrapes. The instruments too, escaped injury.

'It was a miracle!' Lewis stood at the side of the mountain and raised both arms, as if to orchestrate calm and thanksgiving. Moira – dazed, alarmed and breathless – half expected a soundtrack of abrupt violins, the coda out of the violin concerto by Philip Glass. It stayed in her head for two days, even after she had played again.

'It was a fluke!' The driver talked to each of them, and phoned for roadside assistance. Only the stitches on Al's chin and a slight dent in the flare of one trombone remained to remind them anything had happened to mark another long drive to another distant auditorium.

Whatever possessed Moira to accept Lewis's suggestion of a solo accompanied only by Carmen? It must have been a fit of spite. Had she abandoned all sense of fairness and balance? No – it was defeat. It was the kind of hollow vindictiveness that comes from loss. It did not seem like a good idea to be placed in direct rivalry with Oscar, the second clarinet, but even he came forward and urged her to do it. It might all have seemed reasonable if it were not for the accident.

She knew what the driver saw. There was no need for her to crane her neck to look back, even if she had time to do so before the van lurched and teetered for a moment, then crashed over one side and shuddered to an uncomfortable stop against the barrier on the steep side of the road. Had she screamed? She heard voices, and one could have been her own. The groan she heard from Al came later, and it was not due to what he glimpsed when he turned to look, but to the sight of blood on his hand when he wiped his chin.

'Ow … ow.' He protested like a child when she held a fistful of tissues fast to the spot underneath his lower lip where a neat cleft bisected the jutting chin – the very feature that made him so distinguishable, so charmingly good-looking. Perhaps it was not his grey eyes, but his Michael Douglas chin that did it for her.

'Are you all right?'

Then his question was repeated by Lewis. 'Are you all right, Moira?'

'Yes, Lewis – I'll be able to play tomorrow night.' Perhaps she understood them all too well. Perhaps they did not understand her.

It was understandable. Few people remember exactly what happened after an accident. Hardly anyone remembered crawling out from between the seats, calling to each other, screaming, and clambering out of the horizontal door – even the sliding door worked perfectly to let them out.

The van and trailer were replaced quickly with rentals, Al's chin was stitched, the concert the following night was moved back twenty-four hours, and everything returned to normal. But the first trombone headed back to the city. Shaken, he said: he was shaken and would not play until he had had a break.

Lewis let him go with hardly a murmur, which was unlike him. 'Yes, look – all right, Glenn. We'll see you when we get back to the city.'

With Glenn gone, it would have been Al to move up a seat to first trombone, if it were not for his stiff chin. So a recently recruited youngster nervously took Glenn's seat. It all worked perfectly in rehearsals. It worked perfectly until the night of the concert. Moira's number with Carmen solved a lot of problems.

Lewis was adamant. 'It'll be three numbers that Al won't have to play.'

. She could not believe he would sit out the whole band for Al.

It all fell together: Moira finally understood it all, the instant she saw Al's hollow eyes in the wings, the plaster on his handsome chin, and the sadness in the eyes she could not properly see with spotlighting in hers, and a stage manager gently wresting from her hands a bouquet she clung to, in sudden realization.

'Oh!'

She saw Al's lips say, 'One more, Moira!'

She felt her heart miss a beat.

She held up three fingers for Carmen to see.

She played part of the Rimsky-Korsakov concerto. Part: she could not possibly play it all. She would have no breath do play it. There it was in the gloom of the wings, in the darkness bisected by a bright slant from the footlights, what the driver saw in the rear-view mirror. She saw what Al glimpsed when he turned his head a second before the van lurched and they took a tumble that almost sent them down the side of the mountain.

Her breath caught in her chest. How could she do this? How could she play Rimsky-Korsakov without choking?

'One more, Moira.' He mouthed the words to her, lopsidedly, the plaster on his chin moving in the dark. He spoke to her, but his eyes sought Carmen.

Blood had dripped from Al's chin at the accident site, and he brushed it off on his sleeve. Stumbling on loose gravel on the shoulder of the road, Moira watched him paw blindly, and hold on to the rear of the vehicle. How did she not see it then?

'Al? Al – your chin.'

'My chin? Is Carmen all right? Where's Carmen?'

The pianist was sitting on the barrier, holding together a huge rent in her good black pants. 'Look at this!' She laughed, twice, and the high-pitched sound went around the mountain and melded with a siren in the distance. They stopped and listened. It all went so fast. Nurses at a small clinic offered analgesics and sympathy; the staff at the Collarbone Creek hotel were solicitous, wonderful. The police acted like tourist guides. The coffee was the best Moira had ever tasted. Relieved and suddenly a buffoon, the breathalysed driver joined in the impromptu party, and celebrated their close escape with gusto, showing off his ignorance of all things classical, and making them laugh at Irish jokes involving musical instruments.

Glenn was not amused. Moira joined him in a corner, where he nursed a large brandy, deaf to the noise the others made. 'We'll be a bit sore in the morning.' She tried a wry smile.

'I'll be gone in the morning.'

All Moira could do was nod. And shrug. And leave him alone.

How could she have been so blind, so oblivious? How could she not have noticed what Glenn was miserable about? Now that she sensed Al's distance, she thought she understood. Emotion choked her. The stage was not the place to have such a realization. There was nothing she could do but play on.

But the thought of what she would have seen if she had turned her head in the van, just before they overturned, stayed in her head: Glenn and Carmen – sitting together. It would have been entirely normal, completely wonderful, if …

She missed an arpeggio, and knew she had to stop. Carmen would wind up the piece if she gave her a signal. They were so good together: Carmen was a gifted accompanist, who sensed each change of pace, and worked in the soloist's pauses and shifts. If only she had Carmen's gift.

Breath stopped in her chest and she struggled. Anger bubbled to the surface, she felt her face redden, and sweat break out in her armpits and neck. One little rise of her right eyebrow, and Carmen understood. They brought the piece to a premature close. Few would notice – and after all, if they did, they would forgive a curtailed piece for an encore.

Applause broke out. Moira took a deep breath. The place in the wings where Al had stood was empty, but she saw him on the other side. He had walked around behind the curtains and now stood just out of sight, behind the pianist.

Carmen moved, but Moira could not have her stand. She shook her head. Oh no, oh no. She had something to do, and Carmen had to be sitting in her rightful place.

Her pulse raced. This was madness.

She should not do this.

She had to do this.

The lights blinded her, but all those who work on a stage know there is a spot on the boards where the lights beam toward the back. One more step took her to where she could see some of the faces looking up, and they would see her half in shadow. What she had to say needed shadows.

If she looked to her right, she might see two puzzled faces, so she did not look.

When a soloist walked up to the footlights, everyone listened. It was a reaction she knew she would get: silence.

'Ladies and gentlemen – two days ago something happened that I am sure you have heard about. Our van overturned and we all escaped unscathed.'

A few hands clapped, but it was obvious she had more to say.

Moira saw some smiles below her.

'The driver must have seen something in his mirror that distracted him for an instant. It almost cost us our lives - or perhaps worse … destruction of our beloved and valuable instruments.'

There were a few chuckles.

'What did the driver see?' Moira swallowed hard. This was going to be the hardest thing she had ever done. Harder than Debussy's *Premiere Rhapsodie*. Harder than having her favourite clarinet stolen from that theatre in Dubrovnik.

She steeled herself. 'What the driver saw was two people kissing in the back of the van. Two people in love – it made him smirk.'

Some cheered and clapped.

Moira waited. If she looked, she would see the appalled faces of Carmen and Al, so she stared straight ahead. 'Unfortunately, it's not such good news for our ensemble. The couple at the back of the van had no idea their kiss would set off such an unusual chain of events. Because you see, one of them was a married man ...'

The sound she heard was a concerted gasp. They all took breath at once. The silence was palpable.

'... who has since left us, and is now on his way back to the city.'

'Moira!' Al's voice was not hushed, but she ignored it. Neither he nor Lewis would be in time to stop her.

'The other person was a very gifted accompanist, whose work you have enjoyed tonight. And with whom my husband happens to be in love.'

A groan emitted from the audience.

'But it's all turned out well in the end, hasn't it? The first trombone has gone back to the big city to drown his sorrows, and I … I shall play the very last part of the Saint Saens Clarinet Sonata, which has a kind of uplifting melody. It is a rather jolly tune. And it will be my last encore.' She turned to nod to Carmen, who sat at the piano, transfixed.

Moira took a few steps backward, found her place next to the grand piano, and inhaled deeply, and raised her clarinet slightly, as she had so many times before.

It was Carmen's cue. All she could do was play.

Walking into the sea

Leaving

From that day, Ruth had only one aim in mind: to leave the country and look for Dave Havelock. He left some of his books behind. And the pencils. An empty notebook was still on the crate he had used as a bedside table. Ruth used her sharpest pair of scissors and gave herself a haircut the day before she left. She took it off in a straight bob under the ears, stuffed the hair into a plastic bag and threw it into the bin behind the house. So much for that. In the mirror, she looked taller and younger because of her new stark hairstyle. In her grey shirt and old jeans, elastic sided boots and Dave's old jacket, she felt ready for anything. Everything was in bags and boxes on the back of the ute. Ruth stretched the tarpaulin over and checked the house once more. Anyone could get in if they really wanted to, but there was nothing much left inside now. She turned the power off at the mains and got into the driver's seat.

Thinking

Dave's face, shadowed by the sun behind him, turned to look into the kitchen the day he disappeared. 'What I want to draw is not scenery,' he said, his voice making it sound like a joke, 'but the force of nature.' He plucked a pear from the bowl on the table, smelled it, winked at Ruth and walked out. She did not see him again. His pencils were on a fence post a few metres from the far eastern surveyor's peg. One of his drawing blocks was riffling softly in the evening wind. It was as if someone – something – had lifted him from where he sat to draw. But there were clothes and books missing from his room so Ruth knew he was all right. He had just taken off, without saying a word about leaving or distance or regret or the future. Perhaps he had gone in search of water.

Drinking

'If you lower your head and lap from a bowl like a cat,' Ruth told Dave once, 'you will know how it feels to be quadruped.' 'Rubbish!' he answered, but filled a bowl with milk and placed it near the backdoor on the floor. Forgetting she was there, Dave took off his shirt and jeans and went down on all fours, lapping at the milk with ferocity she would remember later. She remembered also the bottoms of his feet, turned out and curled away from him, like a child's feet. She did not ask him how it felt. She backed quietly from the kitchen, entering her room blindly in reverse and closing the door tightly behind her. That night, he turned on some loud music, and said it was a Polonaise. She did not know what that meant. 'Chopin?' But she did not know about that kind of thing. He told her about the sexuality of colour, and how the blue of milk was so female and so subtle it was the strongest of blues. Its taste was essentially distinct from that of water. 'Water tastes metallic – magnetic – because it is so necessary. We need water not only to keep us from dying, but to keep us from drifting away. We are weighted to the earth by water.' Ruth did not always understand him. He would sometimes jump up and illustrate his thoughts for her on paper, scratching lines and swirls on one of his pads. She kept all the scraps, flattening them between pages of a cookery book. She took a sip of water from the kitchen tap that night, to taste what he meant. 'Metallogenicity,' he had said, 'is the origin of it – why everything we depend on tastes of metal.'

Trailing

When she followed him to the dam, she tried to be quiet. But there was a sharp moment when she knew he realised she was following him. They both proceeded in silence, just as before, just as singly. When he reached the dry hollow where there had once been water, he sat on a fallen tree and started drawing immediately. She knew he was scratching colour together. He rubbed yellow, blue and red in a single whorl. He sharpened pencils with a penknife and rubbed them again. 'You need green. You need red and grey.' Ruth knew he was talking to her, but did not move to acknowledge it. She preserved the individual solitude they brought out there with them. Crouching in the bushes, she felt present and not present. 'Green is the colour of silence,' she whispered. She wanted to be surrounded by green, but the country was burnt, yellow. When she squatted to urinate in the undergrowth she made sure he could hear the soft sound of clothing as she drew up her skirt, and the trickle of liquid.

Longing

When he took out the big map she knew Dave was looking for the sea. They were at least four days from it by car. He looked up at her from the table but her face was lost in the dusk light, which was quickly suffusing and drawing backward out of the kitchen door. Perhaps he saw only her silhouette, Ruth thought, only the outline of her body, black against fading blue of the sky caught in the doorway. 'Rocks, sand, saltbush and the sound of green, blue and white in conflict,' he said. The opposite of music, he said it was. He sharpened a green pencil and drew single blades of windswept vegetation on the line of a dune, on a piece of sugar paper on the kitchen table. 'An endless spread without order, is nature.' He drew up his shoulders in a movement she saw as decisive and scraped his chair back on the hard floor. 'The sea is too far away,' he grumbled. She ran the kitchen tap so he could hear water and he pushed her away gently, like a child does at the sea's edge, to dip his head under the flow. Wet as a child from the bath, cold and dripping, he nuzzled her breast. 'I am looking for the sea,' he mumbled.

Moving

Ruth drove towards the coast knowing, because she knew him, where he was bound. She realised she would not return to the house near the dry dam for a long time: perhaps never. The radio voice was dull and sexless, but she heard the word *Polonaise*, and then she was surrounded by the music she could not understand. It was vexing, so she stabbed the button and it stopped. Landscape flattened into plain, swelled into hills and undulations she recognised. Soon, she thought, the sky will become darker over the western horizon and birds will be different ones, with different habits. The clever confidence of birds that live near water, she thought. Near the sea. Dave had taken little apart from books and clothes. Everything else he owned was in the back of her ute. At night, she pushed herself under the tarpaulin and waited for sleep with her back up against Dave's box or Dave's big hessian sack. She wished for a radio that played something other than Dave's music, but the winder was stuck. Daylight made her move. Darkness stopped her in her tracks, making her turn off the road to look for sleep. She drank metallic water out of a dripping bag and thought of Dave tasting salt, days ahead of her.

Watching waves

At the headland, it was like she remembered. There were tiny ships out on the horizon and a straight green line where the sea met the sky. The wind of coasts whipped her newly short hair about her eyes, making them sting.

She heard sea gulls and the moan of constantly rolling waves against the promontory. There were fishermen on the rocks, casting strongly into a steady westerly. What did I expect, Ruth wondered. It was unlikely she would have found him there on arrival: sitting on the rocks and scraping a pencil against a drawing block in the light softened by sea spray. She was not even sure he had headed to this side of the huge bay, whose other flank was miles out of sight to the south. She held a hand to each side of her face to hold her hair away. Tears from the wind rimmed her eyes. Without thinking of the fishermen Ruth let out a shout, a long-drawn yell wrung from her diaphragm. They were too far to hear, and the wind whipped the cry away the instant it left her mouth. Waves crashed somewhere below her to the left. The smell of seaweed and decaying marine life filled her lungs. 'The red and grey of the sea are male. They are the colours of noise and constant feeding,' Dave said to her once. 'Taste the sea and you taste your most desperate longing to be. *Be*-longing.' Ruth walked down to a small shingle beach where a young woman was lying on a blanket with a small child. Wind whipped the corners of the fringed blanket up and the woman tried weakly to straighten it. The baby was asleep, covered with a large beach towel. The mother shielded its face from flying specks of sand. She hummed a tune that sounded far too familiar. With her back to them, Ruth walked to the sea and dipped her hand in the last frothy edges of a retreating wave. Her fingers tasted red.

Arriving

It took Ruth three days to find out whether Dave had been to the seaside town where winter tourists straggled from the pub to the motel and from the rocks to the road and back. At the lighthouse where she was told he went, she found two old men and their story of the war and changes. She listened to as much as she could before asking about Dave. He had walked and drawn pictures, they told her. Pictures he showed them when he returned at sundown. 'Funny shapes and funny colours,' one of them remarked, 'you know – modern stuff where you have to guess the subject.' He winked at Ruth and she turned away, striding out onto the ridge between the sea and the road. From there, grey milling of waves below and sounds of traffic from the highway mixed into the final setting of the sun.

Meeting

She found him at the end of a mole where seagulls squawked and wheeled over their heads. Ruth did not think he heard her approach behind him, awkwardly balancing on huge rocks that made up the breakwater. The shattering of waves was like glass. Bits hit her as she came up behind him. From that day back at the old house, it had become important for Ruth to find him. And now she remembered it. Dave had gone off to draw near the dam, and he was visible from the rise, sitting in the bright sun. She had walked up to him from a place on the rim of the hollow where he could see her. 'It is not easy to fly above places where there is no water,' he said. He had to say it again as she drew nearer. 'Water weighs everything down and lifts it all up again. There is no buoyancy without water.' He had lifted her bodily on that day, pulled her to him and touched her gently without talking. He led her to the middle of the dry dusty dam where there should have been water. He was ferocious and docile at once, a voracious searcher parting dust and water for artefacts, with gentle fingers.

Drawing

Now, he spoke before she was close enough to hear all the words in the wind. '... here we can get wet,' he said, turning to face her, his head forming a shiny halo against the background of breaking waves. He showed no surprise at her arrival, but looked at her short hair and his own jacket wrapped tightly round her body. He hummed the tune the woman had sung to the baby. Ruth thought of slowly sinking into the waves, of grey and red streaks of water sliding onto and off her body. 'Here we can walk into the sea.' he repeated. She saw he had filled pages with drawings. She turned pages of the book, looking for green. 'Everything vital tastes metallic,' she tried to say. She had driven for four days and looked for him for another three. She had searched for red and grey. 'Colour has nothing to do with light, does it?' It was the first question she ever asked him. 'It has to do with weight and taste and sexuality,' she finished in a whisper. 'You don't have to look for water here,' he said. And she knew he was answering her although she saw no connection. 'Even birds know the meaning of buoyancy.'

Walking into the sea

The woman and the baby were no longer on the shingle. The wind seemed to die suddenly. The tops of waves lapped against the small pebbles, shattered into red and grey fragments about her ankles. If she looked at the sky, Ruth knew it would be white. She had imagined it, but she had not found him and he was not there, ahead of her, waist deep in water so cold she could feel its sharpness in her bones. She was alone. She did not think of longing and *be*longing. She constructed a scene. The way he would be if she found him.

The Polonaise he would play, whether she understood it or not. She thought of his boxes and sacks in the back of her truck, the blunt pencils and filled drawing books she carried to him. She filled her pockets with large pebbles and walked out into the sea, lifting her arms to make a ponytail and remembering her hair was now short. She followed Dave into the light of the setting sun. The man was shimmering, like when she imagined him talking to men on the pier. He stopped: a mirage, with a line of green horizon behind him. Lowering his head like he did to lap milk out of the bowl on the floor, he sipped a taste of the sea. She saw his tongue momentarily. A tongue. With her own, she tasted the water. It tasted red, like iron. It was as if her body filled with it. When the waves reached her breasts and buoyancy held her by the waist, she saw him splash and dive suddenly, swimming her way. She dived.

Wetting the stone

Isabel put down the book. It was as heavy in her lap as it was in her hands. The room was cold and made her cramped arms ache slightly. If this is the beginning of arthritis, she thought, but stopped. There was a noise in the yard. She looked through slatted Persian shutters. There was still sun out there and a bright slant distorted red and white tiles. Geraniums in large pots looked dusty and irregular. She had never noticed before, but there was a gap where a pot could have stood sometime in the past. She would look for the circular print of its base when she was next down there.

The noise came again. Isabel scanned the yard. There could be a cat behind one of the flung-open doors, or a bird caught in the loggia across from her window. The loggia was really a huge window, protected by a shallow balcony. Its large coloured glass fanlight reflected the last of the sun into her eyes. She saw it: a pigeon perched on the balcony rail. It had a beautiful green neck like a collar, beady eyes she could hardly see in the remaining glare and an unusual movement in its breast, like a tremor. Or was it quite normal? She had never watched a pigeon before.

Whose soul was transmigrated there, Isabel wondered, and looked at the bird's small head. The words she had just read in the big book stayed in her head. She had traced a finger under the lines that told her of Parmenides, who had a strain of mysticism in his teaching. Like the Pythagoreans, he believed in the transmigration of souls and would not eat the flesh of any animal.

The noise came again when the pigeon fluttered its wings, trying to get away. It had seen her. She flung the shutters open to see better and the bird panicked. Isabel closed them again quickly and walked through the bedroom, the sanctum and the stair landing to the loggia. She tiptoed to the large window and opened it cautiously, but the bird was frantic. It fluttered and flapped, so that she had great difficulty freeing it.

There! It was her second success that day. First, it was the reference to Empedocles, and now, freeing a trapped soul in the body of a green and grey pigeon. She remembered suddenly the white band encircling its eye: a staring eye, one that did not blink.

'I want to choose an animal into which my soul can transmigrate.' She spoke quietly to Leon that evening. He sat in the salon, listening to his operettas, enjoying Lehár. As she walked in, he uncrossed his legs and sat more upright in the white sofa. The fire was blazing and threw orange lights onto the dark paintings that crowded the yellow walls. They were stone walls whose extreme thickness appeared in window recesses. As high as the tall ceiling and over two feet thick, the window alcoves were hidden by yellow damask curtains, drawn at sunset every day. Isabel walked over and started to draw the first pair.

'Karmni will do that.' Leon sounded irritated.

'She can bring us sherry.'

'What's this about an animal?' He looked up from his book, reading glasses bisecting his eyes horizontally. His chin jutted at Isabel.

'Empedocles was a vegetarian.'

Leon sustained his gaze, immobile, indicating there had to be more to what she said unless it was to turn into a banality. Isabel watched his immobility and nearly decided not to speak, to suspend him in his questioning stance forever. 'Do you think pigeons fly about transporting the souls of dead men?' Finally: she had to free him from his belligerence.

Leon did not move his head. Instead he blinked. Then he raised a hand and removed his reading glasses from his immobile face. 'No.' His smile showed her he was going to attempt a joke. 'Storks fly about transporting the wishes of women.'

Isabel frowned. 'Not all women want babies, Leon.'

'Humph.'

'Empedocles invented the notion of four elements...' she tried.

'Or perhaps, discovered it?' Leon blinked. His condescending question was not in the least masked.

175

Isabel gave up. She picked up her heavy volume and put it back on the high shelf from where she had extracted it at random that afternoon. 'Isn't it funny how one can go looking for a thought and find it in any book one opens?' She looked at Leon, who had replaced the glasses on his nose and was about to look down again. 'I know you will have some theory about that,' she added.

'Karmni should bring in drinks any minute.' His mumbling showed defeat of a certain kind.

*

Unlike the Greeks of the mainland, the Western Greeks had no accessible marble suitable for building, but their shelly limestone is an attractive material in texture and colour, and their temples, in severe Doric style, are impressive for their

176

size and proportions; the temple of Olympian Zeus at Acragas
was considerably larger than the Athenian Parthenon.

Isabel put down the heavy book. Why was she so drawn to this ancient stuff? She sat in a cane armchair in the yard, her house walls rising like canyons about her. But this is not Greece, she thought. The red and white tiles radiated diagonally to the walls and met at crumbling angles, shreds and particles of ancient limestone gathered in little dunes on now a red tile, now a white one. Not ancient.

Earth, thought Isabel. Earth on this island does not mean brown clods so rich they stick together into clumps when pressed in a fist. Earth here means limestone slabs, fine white dust and the powder of prehistoric shells filling the thin gaps between masonry blocks.

She rose and touched the crumbling wall. Her palm came away coated finely with limestone dust. There were still patches of whitewash clinging to some parts of the yard wall. It was flaking, yellow, and showed bristle marks of some ancient hogs hair brush. She snapped off a tiny fragment of the whitewash and put it on her tongue. The taste of lime seemed familiar. It was salty, dusty: reminding her of the sea and oysters.

'What on earth are you doing?' Leon was watching from one of the open doors.

'Eating the walls, what else!' Isabel laughed and turned to face him.

He had removed his round distance spectacles and shaded his eyes with the hand in which he held them, dangling from one stem. 'I'd have a glass of milk instead.'

Isabel frowned.

Karmni, the plump maid, came out into the yard carrying an armful of linen. 'You don't want milk, *sinjura*?'

Isabel shook her head and smiled kindly, tilting her head in a way she knew Karmni understood.

Leon moved over and inspected the crumbling wall. 'Time we had these seen to, hmmm? Can't remember the last time the yard was whitewashed.'

'The year of the big flood at Msida.' Karmni's accented contralto filled the space. 'No, no – I remember now. It was the year lightning struck the lemon tree.'

'And which year was that?' Leon's eyebrows were raised.

'The year of the great storm!' The maid smiled as she gave the obvious answer. 'When my sister met that sailor, drenched to his skin. They have four children now.' Her bright smile seemed directed more to the memory of her nephews and nieces than to the puzzlement still visible on Leon's face.

178

'And their youngest is five?' Isabel seemed delighted in the conversation, compounding it intentionally. She returned to her cane seat as Karmni.

'We should arrange for it to be done in a month or so.' Leon was still intent on the walls.

'There are fossils in those walls. I like them as they are.' She rose again. 'Look – see?' Her finger found a faint line in the block of stone where Leon's hand rested. She traced a curve, a spiral.

'Mm. A shell. Most limestone contains shells.'

'I think I *will* have that milk.' Isabel rose from the chair and headed for the kitchen.

He followed her. 'But you rarely drink milk! You never have milk. Not even in your tea.'

'I'm not pregnant, Leon.'

*

Myths were viewed as embodying divine or timeless truths, whereas legends (or sagas) were quasi-historical. Famous events in epics, such as the Trojan War, were regarded as having really happened, and heroes and heroines believed to have lived. In another class of legends, heinous offences, such as attempting to make love to a goddess against her will, or deceiving the gods grossly, were punished by everlasting torture in the underworld.

Fascinating. It seemed so foreign and distant, until one realized many people still believed exactly the same thing.

On the roof, the world seemed golden. The morning sun splashed onto sheets billowing from washing lines strung as high as Karmni could reach on her toes. They snapped like sails in the *Grigal* wind. The walls and floor of the house roof were made of the same limestone, but here it had hardened to rock-hard texture, grey and iron-like, retaining all sharp angles. Karmni stretched washing, pegging it onto wire lines in careful order: sheets with sheets, clothing with clothing, a line of red kitchen towels flapping out of her reach.

'This wind wrecks boats.' She spoke to Isabel without turning from her task.

The tall woman nodded. Looking out over rooftops identical to her own, she blinked in golden light and searched for the line of sea in the distance. The indistinct smudge of an oil tanker broke the horizon.

The maid looked up to a whirring of wings above them. '*Ara kemm hamiem.*' She mumbled to herself. It sounded like a prayer.

Isabel recognised the word for pigeons. 'They turn as one.' She watched the swooping chevron of birds until it became an indistinguishable black speck in the distance over the port.

'They foretell the weather.'

Downstairs, Leon had just come in from his walk. His coat hung over a sofa arm. There was a brown paper bag from the bookshop on the coffee table.

'Funny.' Isabel peeked in the bag as he returned from the sideboard with two glasses of sherry. 'I was reading about myths and legends myself this morning.'

'Picked randomly from the shelf again?'

'You don't believe in coincidences,' she accused jokingly.

He pursed his lips.

'The Greeks took some epics to be true.'

'The Ellises accepted our invitation,' he said, shuffling the mail. 'Here.'

Isabel took the pile of envelopes and sorted out her own. There were letters and catalogues from English book clubs. 'Eternal torture.' She half-whispered to herself.

But Leon heard and tilted his head for an explanation.

'Living in a place where you couldn't receive books would be terrible.'

'So it's not having the Ellises for dinner, then?'

'That's not torture. In spite of their being vegetarians.' She moved into a deeply recessed window to read the rest of her mail, but Leon kept on talking.

'Or in spite of all the little Ellises?' His tone was pointed, piercing.

'I don't mind it once in a while. They are growing.'

'And *Empedocles* was a vegetarian.' His sarcasm cut sharply in spite of his dull voice.

'Leon!'

'You told me yourself.' With his back to her, he sat and read until Karmni came in to draw the curtains.

It was not completely dark outside; Isabel could see into the narrow winding street. The uneven pavement had subsided into layers of bitumen. Built high into a street corner, a shrine with its glimmering lamp appeared ghostlike. It was the statue of a saint, underneath which a plaque in Latin, all but illegible now even to those who could read it, exhorted the faithful to pray, promising days of indulgence from purgatory.

'Two hundred and eighty days' indulgence.' She was flippant, and turned to the room. '*Pater, Ave, Gloria.*'

'That's nine months, Isabel.' Leon stared at her through bisected irises and craned around to look at her.

'Nine months can do other things than gestate a baby.'

Karmni came in, wearing a clean white apron. She announced dinner. She also announced a storm. The

182

Grigal had worsened. Isabel steeled herself for it. Leon turned up *The Merry Widow*. She was sure they could hear it in the street. Perhaps she would bury herself in that book again.

*

Folktales, told for amusement, inevitably found their way into myth. Such is the theme for lost persons – whether husband, wife or child: Odysseus, Helen of Troy, Paris – found or recovered after long exciting adventures. Journeys to the land of the dead were made by Orpheus, a hero who went to Hades to restore his dead wife Eurydice to the realm of the living.

The *Grigal* blew mightily, whistling through overhead cables in streets, past cantonades, and on roofs. It was useless trying to immerse oneself in a book. Isabel held it in her lap and listened. All shutters were secured by Karmni earlier, but Leon went to check them, window by window, pausing especially long at the loggia, where old glass rattled loosely in its frames. Blue glass, ruby glass and glass the colour of honey, cut into segments and set into a half circle over his head. It all jangled and rang. Storm light filtered through and bathed him with jewel colours.

'Must have those panes re-puttied.'

Isabel heard him on her way to the bedrooms. She would turn the electric blankets off. Not wise to use appliances in a storm. She knew he would say that next.

'In the olden days they prayed to Santa Barbara,' Karmni said.

Isabel nodded. The two women went down the stairs together. These ancient limestone stairs, thought Isabel, on which thousands of feet have trodden on layers of fossils, have endured ten thousand storms.

There was an enormous crash from the loggia: smashing and breaking of glass, a particularly ominous noise. The voice of storms. The women screamed at once. In the loggia, Leon's body was covered in shards and knives of coloured glass, remnants of window frame and jagged pieces of old wood bristling rusty nails and hinges.

Wind blew in and swept into the faces of the women as they ascended from the landing. The noise of their voices and the wind was indistinguishable. Everything was covered with dangerous sections of sharp coloured glass, bathed in grey wet light and surrounded by impossible noise. The colour of blood added itself slowly to the wet heap that was Leon's body.

'Santa Barbara!' Karmni screamed. 'Madonna!' Regardless of the danger of cutting herself she stepped into the mess to retrieve her master's body.

184

Isabel tried to contain her panic. She had a sudden insane vision of his soul transmigrating into the body of a pigeon. It flew effortlessly in the gale force wind, gently lifting its wings and swooping into the red and white tiled yard below.

'Help me! Take his arms!' Karmni yelled, telling her what to do .

Isabel seemed paralysed, standing on the edge of the pool of water, glass and blood. Rain blew in over them all through the huge gap that was the loggia.

By the time they got him to the bedroom they were sodden, bleeding and breathless. The lifeless form was draped diagonally on the bed, still bleeding sluggishly from the place where a large sliver of blue glass had impaled him in the neck.

*

In the Archaic period, the dead were better served above ground, by monuments which reflected credit on the living, than below. The few offerings laid with the body were a token of presumed brief need for sustenance, on the way to the other world.

185

The yard walls had not been whitewashed. Isabel looked at the gap in the line of geranium pots and found a rusty circular stain, seeped permanently into the grainy texture of the red and white tiles. It was perfect. She looked up to the whirring of wings.

'Some of them have leg tags,' she heard Karmni say.

The maid stood in the yard door. The women looked up at the birds together; a small flight of homing pigeons perched on the rail of the loggia, restored now over a year ago. It was not ancient rippled glass that reflected grey feathers and staring eyes, but new coloured panes replicating the old ones, firmly puttied into new timber frames. Dusty rain had spattered the glass.

The heavy book lay on the cane chair.

'You have been reading.' Karmni needlessly observed her every move.

'I am going to the cemetery today.'

'But *sinjura*, you have never … you did not even attend the funeral. What is it...?' The plump face was lined with concern.

Isabel picked up the book and sat. 'I must see it.'

'See it?' The maid picked up a tray and hurried away, shaking her head in disbelief.

She does not understand whims, thought Isabel. She thought of the silence after the big storm a year ago, the smell of doused limestone rising from the yard to her bedroom window. She had stood and sat; sat and walked about in the large bedroom for the whole time the doctor was there. She sat immobile for days after that; for the whole time funeral service was under way.

She had imagined friends filing in and out of the church where Leon's coffin was. She had signed bills and cheques, ordering a headstone with a low relief carving.

'Bury him with his glasses,' she had said. 'Both pairs.'

The nuns at the hospital interpreted her strangeness as grief, and had nodded as one, wimpled heads small and black in the white morgue.

'Your children...?' One of them had started to ask, forgetting there were none.

'I am not even pregnant.' Isabel looked into the nun's eyes defiantly.

Later, in the close space of a deep window recess, she regretted the content of the sentence, rather than the way she had said it. She pressed her hand to the glass of the window, looked out into the narrow street and wept onto the stone windowsill, wetting the stone, letting tears seep into the curved line of an ancient shell. She looked down and traced the outline in the darkened stone with a trembling finger. It looked like the illustration of a human embryo.

The music rang through the house. It was possible to have it now. Its sad gaiety would not kill her, after all. The waltz, though, was more than she could bear. She chose a scarf.

'Are you sure you want to go, *sinjura*?' Karmni's concern filled the whole ancient house. The banister rattled with it.

Isabel put on her jacket.

The maid looked querulous. Why a visit to the cemetery? Why now?

She does not understand I need to confirm things, thought Isabel; to make sure it happened. To make sure he is there.

Dancing Words

for Jacques Bouckaert

Nanette could not bring herself to answer the letter. It had seeped words – phrases, whole sentences – over her breakfast table, filling gaps where jars of jam, the butter, and the knife with the yellow handle lay scattered since the morning. The envelope's red and blue trim squared off a patch on which her eye continually stopped. It lay upside down, flap upward, that envelope, as if inviting her to delve further for anything inside she might have missed.

It was a thick letter. She had slit it open hurriedly, as she usually did. Thin sheets of airmail paper were crammed with closely written words. Bright words. They spread over her table like honey, filling the slant of light that fell through the gap in the gauze curtains: danced like motes of dust around Nanette's fair head. She sat, still in the big t-shirt she slept in, head bowed, waiting for the words to settle. Of course they did not: Gerard's words never settled. They whirled about of their own accord, providing meaning other than what he intended as he sat and wrote, somewhere halfway round the world where he preferred to be.

In spite of herself, Nanette let her fingers explore the envelope for more. More than just words. And there it was, a photo of Gerard himself, crooked smile half hidden behind a big goblet of red wine. Like a curious child, she searched the picture for the presence of her brother's wife, Barbara, but she must have been the one who took the photograph. In a corner of the picture, over a small bush of white camellias, Gerard had scrawled *All your brother's love!*

He seemed to be drinking a toast, a celebration of distance.

The dredging of the pond has taken place. It took twenty-four hours to be pumped dry. The bottom was full of mud and silt. Of course the fish were all gone, either frozen or taken by birds. I stripped down to my bathing trunks and waded in to shovel silt away, careful to avoid the water plants. It was almost completely bogged with sodden acorns, algae, reeds: fallen leaves from the autumn oak, which were blackened and turned to sludge. There were frogs, salamanders and insects: prawn-like larvae among the detritus. We filled it again, adding a product to inhibit the growth of algae. All the work we did shows clearly. We installed fifteen fish, and they are now swimming happily among the water lilies, which flower one after the other. Birds come down for a drink and to splash about, frogs jump in and around, and our dog often goes for a little drink. It is clear and bright – a cycle of nature going on in our own garden.

Nanette looked at the words. Her brother's writing was not dissimilar to hers. But how different their situations: he in his European garden, where seasonal changes were almost an extension of his own management of nature's cycles, and she in her yellow apartment overlooking an Australian capital city's main thoroughfare.

She looked through the parted gauze of curtains whose hems she still remembered passing through her sewing machine's rickety pumping leg. She saw lines of trees narrowing down to the bottom of the avenue, where they became a jumble among moving traffic and bustling pedestrians. Those trees had served as her garden for as long as she had been there. She had no need for more foliage, not even an indoor plant. The flat was full of books and plain functional furniture. There was a music stand, of course, and a jumble of sheet music she was always promising herself to organize.

Even the walls were bare. She had painted them herself: a thick butter yellow, and they remained unadorned. She wanted as much difference from their old family home as she could contrive. Gerard's walls, although she had never seen them, were sure to be crowded with artworks of all kinds: definitely a great many from their parents' collection. The only one she remembered with any clarity was the great seascape that had hung over the hall table; a tiny galleon battered by

191

huge seas exactly in the middle of the waves. And there was also a portrait of Napoleon, a copperplate etching gone beige at the edges with strange water stains, brittle and dun coloured like old lace. He must also have grandpa's cello.

Despite the lateness of the hour, Nanette pushed back her unruly hair and took the closely written pages up again. She would have to bring herself to respond to this letter, even though there was nothing to answer. Gerard never asked questions. In all the years of letters, there had been a million full stops, a sprinkling of exclamation marks, but never any interrogation. She looked at the salutation at the end, and turned again to the greeting on the first page. Any stranger reading those lines would have no idea at all it was totally one-sided: that it was the latest of a long line of unanswered letters. Reading it gave no hint at all at what lay hidden behind the dancing words: a carefully disguised plea for response.

Nanette stood and made her way slowly to the bathroom, leaving the riffled blue pages beside crumbs and jars and her plate, beside the knife with the yellow handle. In the bathroom mirror, she vaguely looked at tired skin and her pale ring-less hands, first turned upward, then palms down. It was, she thought suddenly, a most predictably hopeless gesture, so turned away quickly before she could look her refection in the eye.

At the front of the house, the pink rhododendron, which was the only real reason we ever bought the property, is again in a glorious confusion of flowers. Every year we think it must be the best ever. There are also red ones down the side, and purple ones this year. We had – as well! – a great celebration of Michaelmas daisies, which I remember are your cold-weather favourites. Christmas was strange, with all the children away. No one to accompany me on the piano, for the first time. We had a fine flurry of telephone calls on Christmas Eve.

My birthday was marked quietly this year. I have no desire to ritualise my retirement: really it will not happen yet for another few months. We invited no one and received people in the Dutch way, however and whenever they chose to drop in. A visit from our neighbours was very welcome and warm. We are building a gazebo in the garden, so perhaps next year will be different. One of the children may come to stay.

Gerard's letter stayed on Nanette's mind the entire day. She phoned the first violin to say she would not be going in to rehearsals, and wrapped herself in the old striped afghan. Lying on top of her made bed, she twiddled the tuning knob on the radio and played with the television remote control without turning anything on. She feared something familiar might make her feel guilty. She should have been playing, not listening.

Gerard's letter was different this time, but not in any way Nanette could pinpoint. For all appearances, it was just like any of the long letters she received during the last five years, none of which she could bring herself to answer. For a few hours after the arrival of each, she made a tentative decision, a weak resolution, to take up a pen and write a few lines. The feeling was always gone the next day. Months would pass and another letter from her brother would be slit open and read quickly as she moved about whatever apartment she happened to live in at the time. He never wrote expecting an answer: never accused or supplicated. Assuming always she was in the best of health and living exactly as she had chosen to, he never asked questions. For the first time, Nanette wondered what he really thought. What did Gerard think he knew about her, about her life? About her sojourn in Australia, which had become permanent?

Presumably, someone reported her movements to him, her changes of address, because his letters had always found her. They had a cousin with strong family attachments who always knew where everybody was, and she occasionally visited Nanette. How long had it been since Maude's last visit – a year?

The sound of music suddenly flooded the room and Nanette, startled, looked at her own pale hand on the switch. Offenbach: rowdy, spontaneous gaudiness that irritated her. She stopped it as abruptly as it had started.

For all she knew, for all anyone knew, Gerard probably thought she was all alone. Would anyone guess, from the way she looked, from the way the flat looked, that she shared her life with a man? Nanette raised her chin and with eyes level, looked round the room. There were almost no traces of Alec. She smiled wryly. She had referred to him as *a man*. Any man? His side of the room was as bare and neat as hers. His clarinet case was nowhere to be seen.

The breakfast table out there was just visible from the bed. The curtains let in the slant of light that had moved to the right since she had gone to lie on the bed. The jumble of breakfast things revealed the presence of only one person. Alec always rose before her and drank black coffee in a hurry, standing up, before taking off for the theatre or the Llewellyn hall.

From where she looked, the table was at eye level. The yellow-handled knife appeared foreshortened. Light filtered through a jar of honey, throwing a golden shadow on Gerard's letter. There was something in this letter that made her feel different: something she had not noted in any of the others. Perhaps it was because she had read it at leisure, in the quiet of the early morning at the breakfast table, long after Alec had gone.

Nanette looked at the blue pages for a long time. Gerard knew nothing about Alec – perhaps just of his existence, she was not sure. But Alec was there, and in spite of his self-effacing presence, left his mark in the kitchen, buying unusual implements and appliances, cooking ancient recipes he unearthed in hardbound books he bought from an antique shop. He made beef tea, rich casseroles: old-fashioned puddings with thick cream.

Of Gerard's wife, Barbara, she knew only a little more than that: her name. Although he often wrote *we*, he never described Barbara or wrote of her opinions or actions. Nanette struggled to remember her last name and failed. Yet she clearly remembered looking for her when she looked at the photo that morning.

We went to Venice at the beginning of summer. Wondered about the asymmetrical markings on the floor of St Mark's Square as seen from the Campanile. *Wondered at the strangely named streets and alleys, some of which spring up fresh and sudden, confusing orientation, just when one is so sure of one's whereabouts. We listened to gondoliers singing and wondered again, this time about mysterious packages being thrown from a balcony to a waiting sailor, standing in a boat. We stayed at a hotel whose windows were heavily shuttered, but in front of each of which a flowerbox held an impossible quantity of geraniums, all pink and with glossy leaves like stars. Of course there were memories of childhood family holidays on the continent and how you and I had such differing notions of fun and yet were inseparable. I looked at bridges over the canals and narrow waterways where one could touch the walls on either side at once. And there I remembered how we would behave on family holidays, confusing Mama and Papa by demanding simple but unavailable things like Lamingtons, in the middle of Italy! Next year we are going to Rhodes.*

Nanette could not bring herself to answer the letter. How does one write a response to an unacknowledged stream of words that spanned half a decade? It was not possible to take on where there was no leaving off, where there was only current streaming from one side. There was the danger of being overwhelmed by a freak wave.

She moved to the desk between two tall windows overlooking the avenue. No curtains here. Light bathed the whole room evenly; lit up the inside of the desk when Nanette lifted the roll top. What she saw surprised her. A neat array of Alec's things crowded the desk. A matching set of pens she had forgotten she had given him one Christmas was lined across the top, looking as if they were used frequently. Did she know so little of her partner's habits that even this neat display surprised her? To one side were a stack of blank cream paper and matching white envelopes. There was a big lined notepad underneath a sheaf of closely typed papers. A chipped mug held a clutch of well-sharpened yellow pencils.

Nanette dropped the roll top quickly. It slammed shut and hid from her startled eyes the discomforting disclosure – of neatness, care, diligence – that seemed almost embarrassing, like a stranger's nakedness.

A shower and a brisk walk to the centre erased from Nanette's mind any notion of guilt. No thought of incongruity, no thought of lack of intimacy with either her partner or her distant brother was allowed entry as she marched from stall to stall at the market, which seemed to have suddenly planted itself in Parliament Square. Neither brother nor lover was given even mental room as she studied first one artefact and then another. To anyone observing her from a distance, she looked like an eager shopper, perusing goods closely. She lifted a painted egg close to her face and quite suddenly, saw it. Paisley whorls, bright purple and red painted swirls, on the light eggshell: so unexpectedly, that she took a backward step and gasped. The stall keeper smiled., but Gerard's words flooded in again.

We have installed a wood stove in the lounge. It is a Scandinavian fire made of dark metal. Its black cylindrical flue curls to the roof in a pleasant way, which complements the flat white walls. It burns very efficiently, giving us great pleasure and warmth on cold nights when we play jazz cassettes sent to us by Willem. We have a great stack of wood under the eaves at the back of the house, where we found a little sparrow's nest.

198

So we consume the pile in an uneven way, to spare the bird any worry about security – about its home and brood.

Nanette stood by the cleared table and looked down at the paper packet she brought home. A new fountain pen and inkbottle bulged through the paper. She traced the outline of a blank airmail pad with blue pages. Her fingers rustled the paper as she felt the shapes of the newly bought items. Down on the avenue, traffic and people milled and thronged around each other. Nanette saw the plane tree leaves were turning red.

She thought of oaks, of insect larvae, her hand resting on the unpacked pen and paper. Suddenly, she knew what was so different about this last letter of Gerard's. He had mentioned their childhood, he was reminiscing. And that could mean a number of things – all of which were niggling at her. It could be he was simply anxious about ageing. Or perhaps he had some conflict with Barbara or one of his children. He could be in bad health, wondering about his mortality. A mere two dozen months separated them in age: they were so much alike. So different.

She wondered about the hurried way in which she always slit open her mail, knowing instinctively that Gerard had the same habit. She knew the exact way he led his bow. Suddenly, she knew he would sprinkle salt on bread and eat it quickly, exactly as she did. She unscrewed the new fountain pen and looked at its shiny nib. Would she imitate her brother's style, as she would imitate his moods and crazes as a child? She would launch into a description or relate some event, starting with a cursory salutation, as if her letters had been rolling out regularly, through the years. She would not bother explaining places and names, she would not supply unnecessary details, but launch directly into something like a normal response, and the words would dance on the page. As if she had not held off from writing all this time. As if – in fact – all that time had not passed at all. She would have to redress something, bridge something: she would never forgive herself if it were all of a sudden too late. She touched the pen again.

'Yesterday,' she wrote, 'Alec made individual Charlotte Russes. There were sponge fingers and thick dairy cream on the kitchen table.'

The house with its feet in the sea

It stood tall and monolithic, its wood grey with age and salt, and there was nothing else there but sea and sky. It was a solitary house, and from the balcony, Oliver could see nothing else but grey, punctuated by something small on the horizon. He liked to think the house had its feet in the sea. He walked to the railing and touched the wood as he had untold times before, straightened his back, and looked out to the horizon. Past grey waves, past specks of drizzle in the wind, past rolling swell that filled the expanse before him, Oliver peered, eyes blinking and smarting. The sea had always charged him with confidence and knowledge of a kind of control. He knew the sea. He knew boats. It was something that made him different and apart from Celia.

They changed during the early seventies; turned a corner, Oliver thought then. When they moved from the central district to the coast on Port Phillip Bay, Celia and Oliver had been married more than two decades, remaining childless in spite of silly hope nurtured for about ten years. They bought this great house on wooden pillars, and a sailing boat; and began to look outward instead.

Celia resisted the sea. Sometimes, she would sail with Oliver like a guest in his care; gripping a rail uncertainly for the whole time it took him to circumnavigate the grey bay. She saw lighthouses and the occasional dolphin. Once she saw a great sea lion that raised its head and nodded solemnly at her before she had time to point it out to Oliver in the bow.

Gripping a tiller or wheel was akin to holding a pen or wielding a poker at their open fire to him. He was confident on water: confident and perceptive. Celia watched him, entrusting him with her wellbeing and her life whenever she stepped cautiously onto the boards of his boat.

He moored the *Eurydice* a short distance from their small wooden jetty, which was the same age as the house. It bobbed and danced, or pulled docilely at its mooring like an old mare, depending on the weather. Oliver looked out at her, blue hull dark and heavy in the light grey running water. The small tender, a fibreglass dinghy, was either secured to the jetty or laid on its gunnels to one side of the house. He looked at the dinghy now, and thought of paint, barnacle-resistant paint.

He gripped the railing tighter and held his breath. The confidence of the last two decades or so left his body with each breath he exhaled. He resisted exhaling until he felt his face swell and his chest protest. Celia was in the room behind him, behind the large plate glass window, which had protected them from many a bay storm. We have sat behind that glass for so long, Oliver thought. So long we have forgotten everything but the sea and its moods and its caprices. We have watched tankers and liners and sailing craft creep or fly past that window and it is as if we know of no other mode of conveyance here.

Celia valued their car, of course; it was her link with the outside world and friends they still saw. But this house, the house on stilts, on posts thick as his wife's waist, was Oliver's only anchor. It kept him and his typewriter fast on the edge of the bay, his words nearly all of the sea and sailing. He had lost count now of all the sailing articles he had published since they had been there. For the last fifteen years or so, the name of Oliver Stephen was acknowledged as the authoritative voice on matters of the sea.

But today – today, Oliver gripped the railing and surveyed the seascape that spread before him every morning for years, and was beset by a feeling unknown to him; or at least, unknown since his days in the army. It leaked into all his veins, like a foreign liquid substance, spreading and invading his every nerve. It seeped slowly, filling him with an uncomfortable knowledge.

I'm afraid, he thought. I haven't felt fear since I wore khaki, held a gun, smoked cigarettes and drank beer in the mess. I haven't been afraid for years. He released the railing and his hand shook. Avoiding another look at the

Eurydice, he turned and went inside, hand fumbling at the catch on the door. It escaped his fingers and slammed softly against the grey jamb. The noise made Celia look up from her book.

'I've lost it.' Oliver just came out with things when feeling at all unsure of himself.

'Sorry, Darling?' Celia removed her glasses, and her request hung in the air between them.

Although it was only eleven, Oliver strode unsurely over to the sideboard and poured himself a small whisky. 'I'm not sure any more. About anything.'

Celia smiled and tilted her head reassuringly. Oliver only drank before dusk on special occasions; or foreboding ones. They both looked at the glass in his hand.

'I have been sailing for a long time.'

'And writing about it.' Celia nodded for him to continue. Her hand held spectacles in her lap, steadied at the wrist by her other one. She too was disconcerted.

'And now I've lost my nerve.' His voice was gruff. 'I was thinking out there that I just can't go down and take *Eurydice* out.'

'Not today, then.'

'Not today or any other day, I fear.'

Celia shook her head kindly. 'Nonsense, darling. Leave it for a while and devote yourself to your papers and things.'

'Not that either.' When he spoke, Oliver looked down into his glass, noting it was already empty. He set it carefully on the tray and moved slowly to a chair, one that did not look out directly at the bay. He gripped the arms and moved the chair deliberately so he faced away from the window. 'Do you remember when we bought this house, Celia?'

She nodded.

'We marvelled at the great timbers.' He mumbled, half to himself. 'We were amazed at the piers that kept it up and the wharf planks that made the balcony. We stood on the beach and looked at it. Do you remember our disbelief at being able to afford it? And the boat too?'

Celia nodded again and smiled. Perhaps she understood what Oliver was trying to say. Or perhaps she was only appearing to do so, as she had on other occasions whose awkwardness had forced her to stand back and wait for time to pass and take the difficulty away. Celia had a way with difficulty.

'Do you remember,' he went on, 'how pleased we were when we finished paying off the loans and everything was really ours? We went out on the bay with a bottle of champagne and I took you past the cape lighthouse. You wondered about the winding metal staircase inside. You spoke about our own wooden stairs and the sounds the treads make to our footsteps. Up and down.' Oliver was talking to himself. He looked down into his lap, sideways through the doorway to the hall, up at the ship's lamp hanging in the middle of the room. Anywhere except at the window. Then his face hardened.

Celia looked away, then back at his clean shaven face and glaring eyes. 'Perhaps it's something we ate.'

'What do you mean?' Oliver snapped. 'What has eating got to do with it? I'm *afraid*, I tell you! Afraid to take out the boat. Afraid to look out at the waves without holding tightly onto something. Afraid to think what it would be like to take off my shoes and wade...' His voice dwindled off into a helpless whisper and he raised a hand to his forehead. Rising abruptly from the deep armchair, he stumbled in his hurry to the door. His unsure gait had Celia look away sharply to lessen his discomfort and embarrassment.

He turned at the door. 'And I'm afraid of what will happen if I sit at the typewriter now.' Celia could not keep looking away from him, but he knew she did not want to see his face that way. His usually strong features had crumpled.

In 1976, Oliver and Celia went to the Mediterranean, to sail around Sicily and the Aeolian Islands. They rented a small yacht and he took them expertly, in unfamiliar waters, from jetty to jetty. It was not Celia's idea of a change, and certainly not her notion of an enjoyable holiday, but she liked it well enough. She was used by then to clinging to a rail, wearing a life jacket on the calmest of seas, looking forward to the evenings they would spend in some smart hotel, sipping cocktails and listening to a small jazz band. He would wear a white dinner jacket and look very handsome. She took care to find dark cocktail dresses and good shoes that travelled well in the small cases they took.

Oliver appeared in many of the photographs from that trip in his oilskins, or in a striped sailing shirt with rubber buttons and a white studded-down collar. She had taken reels of film, and protected the automatic camera inside her waterproof jacket when the spray flew. Her hair was shoulder length then, and a rich dark brown, tied back out of the way whenever they sailed. Nothing made Celia feel safer and more sensible than a tightly secured ponytail in those days. Oliver was disappointed the day she had it cut, but he quickly became used to the soft waves Celia combed back from her high forehead.

In the bedroom mirror, they looked at each other side by side. Oliver noted she looked at him to see if his morning rage had passed. There still was a deep crease between his brows.

'I am going to walk on the sand,' she said.

'Does that mean you want to be alone, or do you want me to join you, to see whether what I said this morning is true?' His words were intentionally blunt.

'Oh Oliver, there's no need to be so surly.' She turned away from the mirror to look at him but he was already half way down the stairs. In the gathering dusk, soft light from windows facing the bay made the interior of the house blue. The weather was clearing, but the night would be windy. It was a while before she decided to follow the stumbling sounds he made leaving the house.

The little dinghy they kept tied to the jetty was gone when Celia walked onto the sand shortly after dark. The newly risen moon played a narrow band of gold between her and the sky, on the rippled surface of the water.

Somewhere behind her, the slowing hum of traffic from the highway and piano playing from a house on the esplanade reassured her that everything was exactly the same as ever. The sand was heavy and flat, wet and scattered with flotsam from the heavy swell of the last two days.

Celia stopped at a big clump of seaweed and looked down. It glistened in the moonlight and moved slightly. A large green and grey crab pulled the huge mass, struggling in its sideways gait. She looked closer and saw the weed was tangled in the crab's legs.

'You don't really want all that, do you?' Squatting down and trying not to scare the creature, and yet not get nipped in the process, she wove tendrils of weed to and fro, knitting her brow and breathing audibly. At last, the crab was free. It scuttled faster than Celia could stand and step back, and disappeared with a soft swish into the foam.

When she returned to the jetty, the tender was back. Oliver must be back at the house. Usually, she would hear his jazz, from this distance, played loudly on the ageing stereo. There was no music tonight. When she climbed the grey wooden steps that led up to the balcony, Celia saw his dark form and the surprising glow of a cigarette end in the dark.

'You haven't smoked for years!'

'I tried to take the dinghy out.'

210

'Yes.'

'I can't do it, Celia.' Although his features were invisible in the dark he knew she would back away from him and his anger. 'I had to turn back.'

'You haven't turned any lights on,' she said, entering the house.

It was days before Oliver spoke normally again. He had a light growth on his chin and lip, his eyes had calmed. 'We could phone the Barnards,' he said companionably.

Celia looked up from her book and frowned.

Oliver knew he was not going to be let off easily.

'This fear you have cultivated…' she began, her voice chilly and distant.

'It's more like a quarrel.' he interrupted. His fingers scratched at the upholstered arm of his chair. He made as if to get up and make himself a drink. 'I vex you when I drink in the afternoon, don't I?'

'This *quarrel* you have with the sea, Oliver,' Celia took off her glasses and straightened her legs, then crossed them, straight out in front of her, like oars. 'Don't make it a quarrel with me, that's all.'

The sky was black, domed over the house and the sea like an opaque glass hood. When there was no moon,

Oliver liked to stand on the balcony in the dark, waiting for stars to reflect momentarily on the rippled surface of the sea. Tonight, it was Celia who stood out there alone, unusual for her. She did not know whether she regretted not softening her voice, warming in sympathy to her husband's predicament.

Oliver had left the house soon after dinner, and she thought he must be trying the dinghy once more. She thought of the two of them in a dinghy in a little Mediterranean cove, watching distant fishermen shout and gesticulate over a silvery catch, massed and writhing in a big net on their deck. She thought of similarly dark nights, both abroad and at home: her faith and confidence in Oliver's skill in boating, which never gave her a moment's worry, even when he went out alone.

For the first time, Celia felt fear. She gripped the railing, the old grey wood of the balcony, looked out over the blackness radiating from the house with its feet in the sea. She heard the soft swash on sand, waves gurgling around the piers below her. She thought of barnacles and weed clinging to those piers below the surface and thought for the first time about their safety and stability; how she had not given a thought all those years to how the supports and wharf timbers supported them, their home and everything they owned.

Celia listened for the boat, for the sound of oars in the water. She listened for Oliver's return in the dinghy, even though she was not sure whether he had untied it from the jetty and gone out to the *Eurydice*. She could see neither jetty nor dinghy in the dark. Neither was there any part of the *Eurydice* visible in the sombre swift nightfall. She thought of times she had stood in the dark and listened to Oliver's typing, somewhere in the house behind her. It was all silent now. Silent and dark and beginning to feel threatening.

Celia wished she knew where Oliver had gone and how long she would have to wait for him. She moved in the dark to the house and without putting on any lights, went to stand behind the big glass window. Strangely lighter in the house than outside, familiar objects around her made a difference.

How many times have we sat behind this glass, Celia thought. It kept us dry and showed us only what Oliver wanted to see: the sea.

A new fear had entered their lives: fear of the very element that surrounded them, the very substance whose force and threat had its grip on the feet of their house.

Celia could almost foretell the storm by the way she felt that night, behind the dark window. She knew without sign or symbol with what force the wind would lash drops of rain and spume against that window. She knew how the house would sigh and groan as swell pummelled the wooden pillars that had held them suspended above the sea for so long. She knew how the little dinghy, small as half a walnut in the fist of the storm, would pitch and toss in a frantic useless bob; Oliver clinging to its thin gunnels inside it, wet to the skin, shouting his fear into the dark. She knew she had been right to be cautious, to keep aloof from the sea and its seductive power, all those times she sat in the stern of the *Eurydice*.

Oliver was having a quarrel with the sea. And this was its answer: a loud bellowing, a howling bigger than the bowl of dark that settled on the horizon.

'You're not coming back, are you?!' she shouted, behind the pane of glass that shook and shivered from the new wind risen off the water. 'You won't come back now.' Celia pulled her jacket tightly around her and fought the door to go out onto the balcony. It banged shut behind her. In the wet darkness, the howling and booming of waves around her head, she clung to the railing. Its ribs and narrow thin hollows were familiar yet wet, cold and unwelcoming.

She thought of the dinghy tipping, capsizing with Oliver clinging to its sides, shouting in moonless gloom, competing with the claps of thunder filling the bay.

Fatigued and spent as if she had rowed a long distance, wet to the skin from the rain and spray, Celia went back into the house, holding both her hands to wet cheeks. Her hair was whipped about her head, clinging to her skull in clammy disarray. She longed for the security and youth of a tight ponytail swinging against the back of her neck.

The noise of the storm accompanied her inside. She resisted the sea, giving her back to the window. Then she stood shock still. From the back of the house, furtive and cautious at first, came the distinct tapping of Oliver's typewriter.

If you enjoyed these stories, try other collections by Rosanne Dingli:

The Astronomer's Pig
Counting Churches – The Malta Stories
The Day of the Bird

www.rosannedingli.com
rosannedingli.blogspot.com

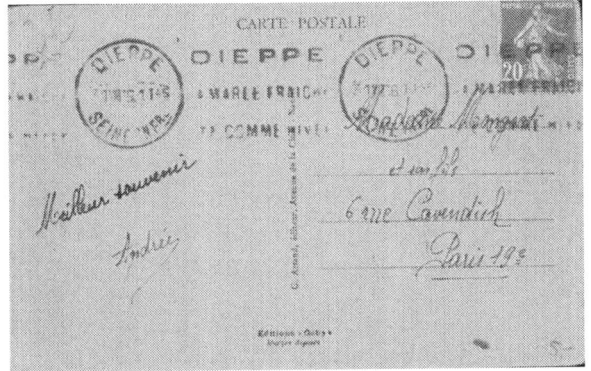

Printed in Great Britain
by Amazon